A KIDS' GUIDE TO

AMERICA'S FIRST LADIES

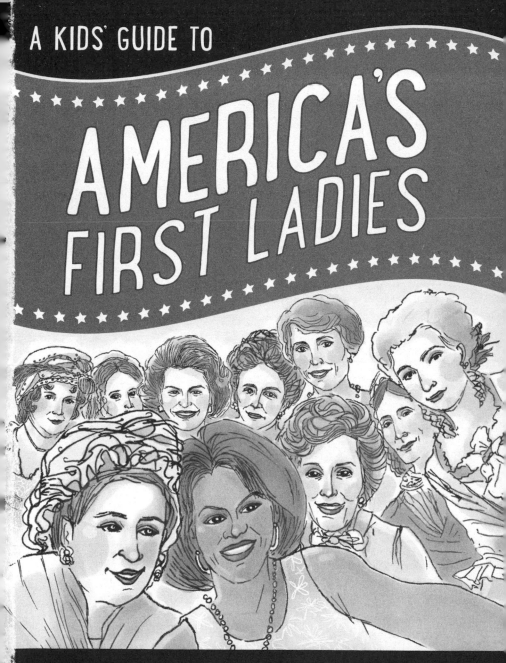

KATHLEEN KRULL

★ ILLUSTRATED BY ANNA DIVITO ★

HARPER

An Imprint of HarperCollinsPublishers

A Kids' Guide to America's First Ladies
Text copyright © 2017 by Kathleen Krull
Illustrations copyright © 2017 by Anna DiVito

Library of Congress Control Number: 2016940933
ISBN 978-0-06-238107-1 (trade)—ISBN 978-0-06-238106-4 (pbk.)

Typography by Chelsea C. Donaldson
16 17 18 19 20 CG/LSCH 10 9 8 7 6 5 4 3 2 1
❖
First Edition

For my first ladies: Cindy Clevenger, Janet Lutz, Lynn Kelley,
Barbara Melkersen, Vicky Reed, and Barbara Patton, and thanks
as well to Sarah Dotts Barley and Pamela Bobowicz
—K. K.

For Su Bick
—A. D.

CONTENTS

Introduction: *First Ladies Rule*   1

Chapter 1. *Must I Always Be First?*
Martha Washington   9

Chapter 2. *Do NOT Forget the Ladies!*
Abigail Adams   19

Chapter 3. *Presidents Who (Technically) Had
No First Ladies and Why*   29

Chapter 4. *Bubbly, Bold, and Brave*
Dolley Madison   33

Chapter 5. *Illness, Heroic Journeys, and Texas*
Elizabeth Monroe, Louisa Adams, Anna Harrison,
and Two Very Different Tylers—Letitia Tyler
and Julia Tyler   41

Chapter 6. *Ambition versus Invisibility*
Sarah Polk, Margaret Taylor, Abigail Fillmore,
and Jane Pierce   57

Chapter 7. *Civil War Breaks Out*
Mary Lincoln   71

Chapter 8. *And Now the "New Woman Era"*
Eliza Johnson, Julia Grant, Lucy Hayes, and
Lucretia Garfield 83

Chapter 9. *The Modern Woman Emerges*
Frances Cleveland, Caroline Harrison, Ida McKinley,
Edith Roosevelt, and Helen Taft 99

Chapter 10. *The Artist and the First Woman Prez*
Ellen Wilson and Edith Wilson 117

Chapter 11. *Flying First Ladies*
Florence Harding, Grace Coolidge, and Lou Hoover 127

Chapter 12. *First Lady of the World*
Eleanor Roosevelt 141

Chapter 13. *Pink and Pretty*
Bess Truman and Mamie Eisenhower 151

Chapter 14. *One Thousand Days—and Beyond*
Jacqueline Kennedy 163

Chapter 15. *A Millionaire, a Goodwill Ambassador, and
One Who Made a Difference*
Lady Bird Johnson, Pat Nixon, and Betty Ford 171

Chapter 16. *The Steel Magnolia, the Iron Butterfly, and
the Enforcer*
Rosalynn Carter, Nancy Reagan, and Barbara Bush 187

Chapter 17. *Developing a Thick Skin*
Hillary Clinton   203

Chapter 18. *The Bookworm*
Laura Bush   213

Chapter 19. *Serious Role Model*
Michelle Obama   221

Chapter 20. *Glamour to Spare*
Melania Trump   229

Chapter 21. *Forty Women Who Shaped America*   235

Selected Sources   239

Index   241

INTRODUCTION

First Ladies Rule

Being a First Lady, the wife of a president, is a weird job. You can tell just by the curious variety in the women who have held the office.

At least two were their husbands' teachers. One was his boss. Others dreamed big or showed brilliant promise—as a concert pianist, architect, politician in her own right, writer of the great American novel—and could have achieved more had they not been so restricted by rules limiting women's lives.

★ ★ ★ ★ ★ ★ ★ ★ ★ ★ ★ ★ ★ ★ ★ ★

ACCOMPLISHED FIRST LADIES

- teacher (many)
- bank manager
- artist
- musician
- dancer
- fashion model
- Hollywood actress
- economist
- department store sales clerk
- geologist, making original contributions to scholarship
- librarian
- businesswoman
- lawyer and law professor
- self-made millionaire
- manager of the family farm
- book editor
- speaking several languages (several)
- mother of children (many)

★ ★ ★ ★ ★ ★ ★ ★ ★ ★ ★ ★ ★ ★ ★ ★

And look at things they've done: One multitasked her way through the American Revolution—packing gunpowder, boosting the morale of the troops, and more. One devoted sixteen years of her life to helping hold a fragile nation together and making Washington, DC, a proper capital. Another shepherded her young son on a frightful forty-day journey across war-torn Europe. Deciding that her destiny was to run the country, one yanked her husband up the ladder with her. One encouraged her husband to go on diplomatic missions around the world and was delighted to join him every step of the way. Another didn't hesitate to take over the reins of government when her husband fell ill, with at least one direct effect on history. Still another buzzed all around Chicago in her Mercedes-Benz, learning how to solve people's problems.

Many traveled and represented their husbands with great skill. One bravely took a train trip to campaign alone, facing hecklers with aplomb. Another dazzled people with her air of mystery and glamour and the way she researched each place she visited. Several were courageous ambassadors of goodwill, soaring into earthquake disaster areas, combat zones, and other hazards.

But what exactly is a First Lady supposed to do? There's no job description in the Constitution or anywhere else.

She isn't the chosen one—the one who got elected. On the other hand, she usually had a lot to do with the victory.

Once she moves into the White House, she has a staff to do all her household chores. But she also might be working harder than she ever has in her life. The country—

and the world—are watching her every move. The public expects her to be a dynamite hostess, a motherly figure, a role model, a style icon, an adoring wife with perfect hair and perfect children, and so much more.

It's stressful. Some women cry on the day they arrive in the White House, while some hold their tears until the day they leave—crying in relief.

★ ★ ★ ★ ★ ★ ★ ★ ★ ★ ★ ★ ★ ★

Ways They Made a Difference

- One personally played a role in adding on our second-largest state.
- Another influenced what was perhaps the most important and controversial piece of legislation in our history.
- One, possibly the most beloved woman of all time, played a part on the world stage, helping countless others.
- One changed people's minds about big topics, like cancer and addiction.
- Quite a few were more popular and appealing than their husbands and were the decisive factor in their winning the election.

★ ★ ★ ★ ★ ★ ★ ★ ★ ★ ★ ★ ★ ★

And it can be really awkward. A woman has been First Lady of the United States since 1789, when our government was founded, and yet for many of those years women couldn't vote or own property or go to college or work outside the home. Meanwhile, a First Lady is a woman who suddenly has a huge amount of power to shape opinions on culture, child care, books, and much more.

Many will criticize a First Lady no matter what

she does. She can have a hobby or volunteer for an uncontroversial cause, but working outside the White House is discouraged. She's not *supposed* to meddle in her husband's business—of running the country—even if she has some pretty good ideas. And if she attempts too much, she risks ridicule, condemnation, even death threats.

Oh, and she doesn't get paid.

Each First Lady has to craft her role all on her own. Some had help from cozy relationships with supportive spouses who cheered them on, but others did not. Often they influenced one another, searching for role models in the women who came before them and giving advice to those who followed.

They all became hostesses, though—some were better at it than others. Some women had terribly hard lives, limiting their energy and fearing the White House as a prison. Others kicked up their heels and threw themselves into their role, knowing that their parties could aid the president's relations with other countries and leaders.

THE TITLE

The wife of a president had no official title at first—just "wife." Martha Washington was often called Lady Washington, and a newspaper article once called her First Lady, but the term took years to catch on. Some historians think that Dolley Madison was hailed as First Lady at her funeral in 1849, and it seemed to gain traction after that. Admirers of Lucy Hayes called her First Lady in 1877, and by the 1930s it was in common usage.

★ ★ ★ ★ ★ ★ ★ ★ ★ ★ ★ ★ ★ ★ ★ ★

Ways to Get Out of Hostessing

- be too ill to leave your bedroom
- raise silkworms
- write poetry
- play piano and harp
- read tons of good books
- write letters to your dead son
- go horseback riding, or to the ballet or theater
- play with grandkids
- hold séances
- crochet 3,500 pairs of slippers

★ ★ ★ ★ ★ ★ ★ ★ ★ ★ ★ ★ ★ ★ ★ ★

Most First Ladies have had special causes they cared dearly about and poured all their energy into. It seems odd today, but several of them—repressed by the conventions of their times—opposed the right of women to vote or make advances. But others did as much as they could for women's rights, trying to break or at least loosen the rules.

Most of them acted as their husbands' eyes and ears, helping invisibly behind the scenes.

And *each one* had an impact on American history. Here, presented chronologically, is a galaxy of some of the most intriguing women of all time—the ones who helped shape our country.

FIGHTING FOR OTHER WOMEN

- One pleaded with her husband to "Remember the ladies!" and did her best to ignore his laughter.
- One of our sickliest, ghostliest First Ladies was the first to publicly support women's right to vote.
- When one found out that the woman on her husband's team of doctors was being paid half what the men got, she made sure that got fixed.
- One raised money for a medical school—on the condition that it admit women.
- Despite her husband's disapproval of women who worked, one insisted on having receptions on Saturday afternoons, so women with jobs could attend.
- One helped to inspire the birth of what became known as the women's movement.
- One was so passionate about political appointments going to women that her husband's administration set a record.
- "Well, what did you do for women today?" one asked her husband every night.
- One made women's rights central to American foreign policy.

CHAPTER 1

Must I Always Be First?

Martha Washington

Martha Washington (served from 1789–1797)

Martha Washington (1731–1802) might have had it the toughest. She had *no one* to tell her what to do when she became First Lady.

But she was smart—with a better education than most women in Virginia—plus brave, a great listener, and compassionate. Above all else, she was a patriot. She was part of the revolution that broke the thirteen colonies away from Great Britain and created the United States of America. Martha lived in a constant state of suspense—there was no guarantee that America would win its war for independence, much less endure in the years after. But nothing was more important to her than staying true to the American Revolution's spirit.

She was brought up as a wealthy girl, skilled at riding horses. Besides being taught to read and write at an early age, she learned all the domestic arts of how to keep a family happy. She was an avid letter writer and an avid reader—she favored the Bible, but she also ate up Gothic romance novels.

When her first husband died, she was the twenty-six-year-old owner of more than 17,500 acres of land and nearly 300 slaves. He hadn't left a will, which would have automatically transferred the property to another man. When she decided to remarry, it would all go by law to her new husband. So for a time she capably ran the five plantations left to her, bargaining with merchants for the best tobacco prices, shrewd about getting advice—while raising her two children who had survived infancy.

As a rich widow, Martha was more independent and more capable of choosing her own destiny than just about any American woman of her day. By the time she met George Washington, she was much wealthier than him.

So she took her time getting to know George before deciding to marry again in 1759.

The decision wasn't all that hard. George was eight months younger than her, but one foot and two inches taller—at six foot two, standing head and shoulders above most men. His reputation as a heroic military leader in the French and Indian War (1754–1763) as well as being an ambitious political figure in Virginia more than made up for his lack of money. He was a kind, fatherly figure to her two children. He was sincere and stylish, had charming manners—the complete package.

★ ★ ★ ★ ★ ★ ★ ★ ★ ★ ★ ★ ★

Heartbreak for Martha

In Martha's time, children were terribly vulnerable to disease and death. Only half of all children reached the age of five. To treat her own children's illnesses, Martha used the usual remedies of her day and also invented some of her own. For pinworms, which she saw as the cause of most childhood illness, she brewed rhubarb and cloves of garlic with the best wine or whiskey she had on hand, doling the potion out by the teaspoon. Alas, she ultimately outlived all four of her children.

★ ★ ★ ★ ★ ★ ★ ★ ★ ★ ★ ★ ★

We don't know many details about what George and Martha thought of each other. He called her a "quiet wife" with a "quiet soul," and with her quiet ways she assisted him in everything he did. When he was appointed commander in chief of the Colonial army in 1775, she made the difficult journey to his camp, wherever it was, for the eight long years of the American Revolution. She faced all dangers with courage. She had a fear of boats, for example, but forced herself to get over it. When smallpox was cutting down George's troops, she set an example for them by getting the smallpox vaccination herself, even though it terrified her.

She stayed with him for months at a time, though they were allowed only an hour alone every morning, when everyone was told not to disturb them. Under the stress of leading his poorly equipped soldiers against the mighty British military, George had no one he could be himself around, except Martha. He confided in her and asked for help in solving all problems.

He wasn't the only one who depended on her to keep his spirits up. The beleaguered, weary troops saw her as a beloved mother figure who spent time with them, singing the popular tunes of the day, chatting, and drinking tea. When some soldiers wanted to give up and desert, she helped keep them united in their efforts.

Martha took the lead in getting other women to switch from doing useless fancy embroidery to knitting supremely useful wool socks for the soldiers. They churned out an endless supply. She also organized groups of women to make bandages, pack gunpowder into precise amounts for loading into guns, nurse the injured, help the families left behind, and do whatever else they could to help the cause.

Whenever she arrived at camp and saw the troops welcoming her, she got her reward: "I felt as though I were a very great somebody." The British hated her and at least once threatened to take her hostage.

Once the war was won and General Washington was the unanimous choice for the world's first elected president (no campaigning necessary)—everything changed. They moved to New York City in 1789, then to a mansion in the temporary capital of Philadelphia.

Martha was well aware that, assuming the new country survived with more presidents to come, her behavior would become the model for their wives. She had to step carefully.

Could she flee back to their lovely estate in Mount Vernon, leaving the new nation's leader on his own? No, not an option.

Could she just hide in her room? Also not an option.

Should she wear a crown or have a fancy title? Should she grow conceited with all the praise heaped on her and George? No, any hint of acting like royalty in a European court, with its rigid hierarchy, was out. Her challenge, in this new democracy, was to remain down-to-earth and treat everyone equally no matter what their social status.

Martha's solution was to provide access to the new president with a public reception every Friday night, open to anyone as long as they were nicely dressed. At the presidential mansion, members of Congress, visiting VIPs, and ordinary people from the local community were presented to Martha, seated on her couch. After curtseying or bowing to her, they got to have refreshments (wine, tea, lemonade, rare fruits like pineapple or coconut), mingle, and talk with the president.

Over the next eight years Martha held a dinner party every Thursday. She invited mostly men—government officials and foreign dignitaries. These dinners could be awkward. Some men were too shy to speak. Others felt that good manners were unbecoming in a real man, and made a point of being rude when they didn't know or like one another. Martha used her friendly ways to get them to relax and kept conversation going as best she could.

NOT A FRUMP

We think of Martha as dowdy, not making as much of a statement as did George. But in fact she liked beautiful clothes and ordered them from England (of course, not during the war) and had something of a shoe obsession. At their wedding she wore amazing high heels of deep purple studded with silver sequins. She typically bought six new pairs of shoes each year. George ordered them for her—once even a pair of "satin pumps embroidered with gold."

She could talk to anyone about anything. She read all the newspapers and magazines and was very well informed. Men were often surprised at her considerable knowledge of war and her patriotic fervor—unexpected traits in a woman. She was never uncomfortable in an all-male group.

One trend she couldn't help but start was that of being criticized no matter what she did. Sometimes she was mocked for being too regal—she had grown up wealthy and her manners were more formal and gracious than the average person's. Other times people judged her too common—she always hustled herself and George off to bed promptly at nine, which was considered an uncouth hour to exit.

But those who knew her genuinely liked her. They appreciated how mellow she was—not at all haughty. Even

Abigail Adams, wife of the vice president, found Martha "modest and unassuming, dignified and feminine." Abigail was critical of just about everyone, but praised Martha: "A most becoming pleasantness sits upon her countenance. And an unaffected deportment which renders her the object of veneration and respect."

Still, weeks into the presidency, Martha wrote, "I have not had one half hour to myself since the day of my arrival." She didn't like to complain, but she was unhappy: "I think I am more like a state prisoner than anything else, there is certain bounds set for me which I must not depart from." Daily routine as the president's spouse was a bit dull after all the hurly-burly of war. But Martha *never* shirked her duty, putting on an act of enjoying herself that convinced all around her.

★   ★   ★

WISE WORDS
"I am still determined to be cheerful and happy, in whatever situation I may be; for I have also learned from experience that the greater part of our happiness or misery depends upon our dispositions, and not upon our circumstances."

★   ★   ★

The only thing that really excited her was helping war veterans as much as she could. She gave them cash, traded stories, got them out of legal jams, and urged her husband to give pardons when necessary. Any vet who came to see George and was unable to was thrilled to see her instead.

She continued to keep George's spirits up. As a couple, they loved going to plays, even ones that were considered scandalous for ladies, and went to every display of anything unusual or bizarre, like zoo animals or a wax museum.

MARTHA AND SLAVERY

Her cake recipe required five pounds of flour and forty eggs—but it was slaves who did the actual work of making it, as with all her chores. Both Washingtons grew up in a racist culture, blind to the hideous contradiction between the ideals of the new America and the idea of enslaving other human beings. George sort of evolved—he turned out to be the only Founding Father to free some slaves while he was alive, instructing that the others be freed after Martha's death. But Martha grew up believing that slavery was part of the natural order of things and never changed her mind. When slaves who she believed she was treating well made their escape to freedom, she was genuinely shocked.

After years of being in the public eye, the Washingtons were able to retire to Mount Vernon in 1797: "The general and I feel like children just released from school," gloated Martha. They enjoyed a little leisure amid a constant stream of visitors paying their respects.

After George died in 1799, she never really bounced back from the end of her thirty-nine-year happy marriage. She died two years later, at age seventy, of a severe fever.

Before she died, she did do history one disservice. She burned all their private letters. It was a custom for some people then, wanting to preserve their privacy. But in this manner she cheated historians out of learning more about her role as First Lady, which might have been greater than we know.

Still, she lives on. In a 2014 poll of historians and scholars, George and Martha were ranked as the country's second-most-effective power couple (after Franklin and Eleanor Roosevelt).

Martha Washington, all on her own, set a standard for future presidential spouses to live up to. It would be hard to find women to walk in her sparkly shoes.

CHAPTER 2

Do NOT Forget the Ladies!

Abigail Adams

Abigail Adams (served from 1797–1801)

"You will either make a very bad or a very good woman," a family friend told her. That's how rebellious Abigail Adams (1744–1818) was as a girl— the perfect personality for the rebellion she would be part of as an adult.

She lacked a formal education and was always bitter about her male relatives having more than her. Contrary to everybody else, she thought women's brains were just the same as men's. Alive with curiosity, she read everything she could get her hands on and made herself into one of the best-educated women in the colonies by the time she was seventeen.

Young John Adams, a Harvard graduate launching a career in law, was impressed with her extensive reading—and everything else about her. Calling her "Miss Adorable," he wrote her love letters demanding that she "give him as many kisses and as many hours of your company after 9 o'clock as he shall please."

After their marriage in 1764, their letter writing was to become its trademark. Long separations kept Abigail from her husband while he traveled as a lawyer, and then emerged as one of the country's top leaders. She stayed behind at their home in Massachusetts while he represented their state at meetings of the Continental Congress in Philadelphia, hashing out the details of how the new country would be governed.

He also traveled to Europe trying to get other countries to help. Abigail begged him to take her along on his sea voyages, but he was aghast at the thought of her being less than perfectly groomed on board. "No being in nature is so disagreeable is a lady at sea," he said.

By all accounts John was difficult to get along with, and when he was home Abigail put up with his prickly personality. But mostly, she struggled alone to raise four children and keep the family farm going. She knew how to make her own soap and candles and everything else about a well-kept household. She managed their money, struggling with wartime shortages and high costs, and had an escape plan in place in case of attacks by the British. When her children's formal education was interrupted, she homeschooled them and did it well, with one of them, John Quincy, showing great promise. She dealt with tragedy, like the death of her baby daughter, and never complained, never played the damsel in distress.

"I think I am very brave upon the whole," she wrote of all she endured.

★ ★ ★ ★ ★ ★ ★ ★ ★ ★ ★ ★ ★ ★ ★

ABIGAIL AND SLAVERY

Going way against the grain, Abigail was an ardent abolitionist (as was John, unlike all the other Founding Fathers). She simply believed that slavery was morally wrong. She saw right through the hypocrisy of breaking free of the British while still owning other people, believing that we "fight ourselves for what we are daily robbing and plundering from those who have as good a right to freedom as we have." She often had servants, who she paid, but never owned slaves.

★ ★ ★ ★ ★ ★ ★ ★ ★ ★ ★ ★ ★ ★ ★

On top of all her responsibilities she found time to write John letters, as many as three a day, about what was going on in the Massachusetts colony, about the necessity of breaking free of Great Britain, and about what he should be accomplishing in his jobs. She had become very interested in politics, read everything being published, and utterly supported the cause of America's independence. Her letters were witty and detailed, the best record we have of some forty crucial years in our history.

Abigail is most fondly remembered for the letters she wrote to John during the Continental Congress as he worked on the Declaration of Independence.

★　　★　　★

WORDS WORTH REPEATING

"In the new Code of Laws which I suppose it will be necessary for you to make I desire you would remember the ladies, and be more generous and favorable to them than your ancestors. Do not put such unlimited power into the hands of the husbands. Remember all men would be tyrants if they could. If particular care and attention is not paid to the ladies we are determined to foment a rebellion, and will not hold ourselves bound by any laws in which we have no voice, or representation."

★　　★　　★

As much as John normally used her opinions to help shape his own, this time she was too far ahead of her time to be taken seriously. The whole topic was humorous, and he joked about her being too "saucy."

She came right back at him with more words that became famous: "While you are proclaiming peace and goodwill to men, emancipating all nations, you insist upon retaining an absolute power over wives. But you must remember that arbitrary power is like most other things which are very hard, very liable to be broken."

Abigail had opinions almost no one else was voicing. All the laws were against women, and she sought for ways to change this. Her solution was to provide more education for girls: "If we mean to have heroes, statesmen, and philosophers, we should have learned women. The world perhaps will laugh at me, and accuse me of vanity." At a time when most people believed that education ruined a woman's chance to have children, writing letters was as far as she could go with her opinions.

Eventually, just before John was appointed minister to Great Britain in 1785, Abigail joined him, spending four years in Europe, making her even worldlier and more knowledgeable.

Few people were as patriotic as Abigail. During the war she boycotted English tea and made her own dresses or wore old dresses instead of buying English fabric. She put on a brave face while enduring the absences of her husband: "I find I am obliged to summon all my patriotism to feel willing to part with him again. You will readily believe me when I say that I make no small sacrifice to the public." All the while, she pointed out that laws rewarded men for their patriotism—but this was not the case with women, which made them all the *more* heroic.

At least when the country rewarded John with the presidency, she would get to live with him, joining him in the new capital of Washington, DC. But the city wasn't a city yet, just a swampy wilderness. And life there wasn't going to be fun.

★ ★ ★ ★ ★ ★ ★ ★ ★ ★ ★ ★ ★ ★

The White House Then

The Adamses were the first family to live in what came to be called the White House. It was still under construction, being built by African Americans, both free and enslaved. It wasn't glamorous—Abigail called life there a "splendid misery." It had no indoor bathrooms, a water source five blocks away, and only six livable rooms with inadequate heating. They brought their own furniture and took it with them when they left. They had four servants, and Abigail did some chores herself, like hanging the laundry to dry in the reception area where every caller could see their underwear.

★ ★ ★ ★ ★ ★ ★ ★ ★ ★ ★ ★ ★ ★

Becoming First Lady was unnerving at first. She asked her two sisters to warn her anytime she was behaving too much like a queen. She also peppered Martha Washington with questions about how to act. "You know inside yourself how to behave" was Martha's ambiguous advice. Despite the less-than-ideal circumstances, Abigail dutifully held dinners and receptions and lived up to Martha's reputation over her four years.

She was always calm and optimistic. Sometimes she even wondered if she was stupid because she genuinely liked to keep those around her happy, constantly soothing John's anxiety, and felt tranquil even in the midst of her turbulent times.

John still considered her his most important adviser. She attended debates on the floor of the House of Representatives and discussed everything with him. He valued her brain. With the most brilliant men in the country advising him, Abigail was proud that he listened to her above all. She was much bolder than Martha about giving her opinions. For this many mocked her as "Mrs. President," considered a most unflattering thing to say.

Women Who Influenced Abigail

Role models for Abigail were few and far between. One was Lady Catharine Macaulay, a famous scholar in England, one of the first woman historians. Abigail was crazy with curiosity about her and how she managed to accomplish all she did. Another was her friend Mercy Otis Warren, one of the first American women to publish her writing. Later, Mary Wollstonecraft's *A Vindication of the Rights of Woman* (1792) electrified her—it was one of the very first expressions of feminist thought.

Financially Abigail ran a tight ship, making sure they kept enough of John's presidential salary to invest for their retirement. After they left office, she mourned the loss of her influence: "My power of doing good to my fellow creatures is curtailed and diminished."

She remained keenly interested in political affairs for the rest of her life. She died at seventy-three of typhoid fever, not living to see her son John Quincy become the sixth president.

The Adamses were most well-known for their letters, which have made a great contribution to presidential history. Abigail was very well aware of the letters' value to history and saved them all—eyewitness accounts of the home front during the American Revolution, bold political advice, and the first pearls of wisdom about women's rights in America.

In her day, Abigail was a rebel. And today many people's favorite First Lady of all.

CHAPTER 3

Presidents Who (Technically) Had No First Ladies and Why

Some presidents didn't have a First Lady to stand beside them. They didn't have a partner to help run their household, a wife to cater to their needs, or a gracious hostess to prepare and run their events. While some of these tasks were left unheeded, the role of hostess was one that did need to be filled, and so relatives and family friends pitched in.

Thomas Jefferson (1801–1809): Weakened by childbirth, his adored wife Martha died in 1782 at age thirty-three after the last of her seven pregnancies. He never remarried. Believing that official events, to be proper, required a hostess, he established the precedent of asking a woman, usually a relative, to help out. In the White House he relied on his daughter, Martha Jefferson Randolph (who had twelve children), to act as his unofficial First Lady and hostess, as well as his secretary of state's wife—the popular future First Lady Dolley Madison.

Andrew Jackson (1829–1837): His beloved wife, Rachel, died three months before he was inaugurated, and he also never remarried. For hostessing duties, he relied on his niece, Emily Donelson, and his daughter-in-law, Sarah Yorke Jackson.

Martin Van Buren (1837–1841): His beloved wife, Hannah, died in 1819 at age thirty-five, after six pregnancies in twelve years. He, too, never remarried. His daughter-in-law, Angelica Van Buren, was his hostess from the age of twenty-one, the youngest woman to serve in the role.

James Buchanan (1857–1861): The only president who never married, he depended on his niece Harriet Lane Johnston as his hostess.

Chester A. Arthur (1881–1885): His wife, Ellen, died two years before he became president, and he relied on his sister, Mary Arthur McElroy, as his unofficial First Lady.

CHAPTER 4

Bubbly, Bold, and Brave

Dolley Madison

Dolley Madison (served from 1809–1817)

Dolley Madison (1768–1849) was one of our flashiest First Ladies, a patriot who used her superb social skills to help the country.

Dolley's background was unusual. She was raised as a Quaker, a religion that holds men and women to be equal and deserving of the same education. With that kind of start, she grew into one of the best-read people in the country. When her father's business failed, her mother rose to the occasion and opened a boardinghouse for politicians visiting Philadelphia, which Dolley helped to run.

Her father picked out a husband for her, a nice young Quaker lawyer. Alas, he died in an epidemic of yellow fever that also killed their new baby. She was left a twenty-five-year-old widow with a young son to take care of.

A few months later, James Madison asked her out on a date. James was a Virginia congressman and a VIP Founding Father: more than anyone else, he was responsible for drafting the new U.S. Constitution, particularly its Bill of Rights. He was two inches shorter than Dolley, seventeen years older, shy, and very quiet. But she grew to like him—and his ideas. She and her son joined him at Montpelier, his beautiful Virginia estate of two thousand acres with some sixty slaves that kept it running.

James was all brain, not warm and fuzzy. Dolley was the exact opposite—a total extrovert, with social graces to spare. It was impossible to find a person who didn't like her, and she succeeded in making James more likable. Even Thomas Jefferson, who loathed the thought of women in politics, liked Dolley. He asked her to be his hostess during his presidential term, while James served as secretary of state.

So she had some practice by the time she got to the White House with James. Possibly more than any other First Lady, she reveled in her role—and there was a lot for her to do.

The country was still very fragile, with many thinking it could break apart at any time. Another war with England—the War of 1812, sometimes called the Second War of Independence—loomed. Dolley saw her goal as establishing unity, keeping squabbling Americans all united against a common enemy.

It took all her creativity. Over her eight-year term, she hosted "Mrs. Madison's Wednesday Nights." The evenings were also known as "squeezes" because so many squeezed in to meet her and her husband. Anyone could come, and they did—two to three hundred people regularly, and as many as five hundred by the time the War of 1812 broke out. Her parties had more laughter, yummier food, and more gossip than previous White House events. They were her way of reassuring a frightened nation that James had everything under control.

No president before or since has been so accessible—which was all the more startling because James was so shy.

Dolley also hosted more dinners than any First Lady before or since. She would sit at the head of the table and direct the conversation wherever she wanted to take it. She was famed for serving delicacies like ice cream (laborious to make, requiring lots of ice—her favorite flavor was oyster). Her dinners were so elegant they could get people to overlook what a primitive place Washington still was to live in.

Always her goal was for people to get along, and in an era when fistfights and duels were all too common, she had a knack for soothing quarrels. Hostile statesmen, prickly envoys from other countries, warrior chiefs from the West, flustered young people—she welcomed everyone and got them to see one another as human beings.

★ ★ ★ ★ ★ ★ ★ ★ ★ ★ ★ ★ ★ ★ ★ ★ ★ ★

DOLLEY'S BAD HABIT

Some were shocked by her use of rouge and other cosmetics that were considered sinful. But even more looked askance at her use of snuff, a tobacco sniffed up the nose. It was a little crude, something women didn't do, but Dolley was addicted. She always carried a gold snuffbox with her and would delicately dip her finger into it, carrying two separate handkerchiefs for cleaning her nose. Yet even this had a political purpose, as when she shared her snuffbox with men she wanted to cultivate.

★ ★ ★ ★ ★ ★ ★ ★ ★ ★ ★ ★ ★ ★ ★ ★ ★ ★

One of our shorter First Ladies, she made herself the tallest person in any room with colorful turbans into which she stuck brilliant feathers. Fashion was important to her goal—wearing the finest clothes money could buy made her a magnet for attention. She became the most popular person in the country, capably transferring that attention to James. Even her parrot, Polly, who could swear in French, was famous.

It was part of her strategy to report to James any news or gossip that could help him. He greatly valued her political advice (and at least once he said women should be educated on an equal basis with men—which was not the common attitude). She didn't take public stands on controversial issues but was extraordinarily well-informed. She kept up with the news by letter, newspapers, and constant visitors, and she attended any sessions or hearings that were open to the public, encouraging other women to join her.

She anxiously followed the war news, but like everyone was caught off guard when the British attacked Washington in 1814. Most assumed the troops would head for Philadelphia or Baltimore or someplace more consequential. She had to flee the capital on her own with her slaves, grabbing James's important papers before she left. Most famously, she also grabbed the portrait of everyone's hero, George Washington, an act that made her into a national heroine. The British arrived shortly after and set the White House on fire.

★ ★ ★ ★ ★ ★ ★ ★ ★ ★ ★ ★ ★

DOLLEY AND SLAVERY

No record exists of what she thought, but her actions make it clear that she went along with the view that slaves were less than human. She was raised a Quaker, a religion that forbade slavery—at one point her father freed all his slaves, then had an impossible time supporting his family. But when she married James, who hated slavery but depended on it to keep his plantation running, her Quaker beliefs seemed to go out the window. When he died, James left his slaves to Dolley, ordering that none was to be sold against his or her will. But she disobeyed, instead selling them as she needed the money to pay off debts.

★ ★ ★ ★ ★ ★ ★ ★ ★ ★ ★ ★ ★

With the White House burned down to a hollow shell, the Madisons moved to the Octagon House a few blocks away. Dolley barely missed a beat in hosting her parties. They seemed more necessary than ever—especially after the war ended in 1815 and the country could celebrate independence once more. The United States was now officially a world power.

Besides partying, she supported many charities, including the Washington City Orphan Asylum. Caring for orphans was a noncontroversial way of using her power, and she threw herself into the work: "I never enjoyed anything so much."

★   ★   ★

WAYS THAT DOLLEY HAD TO APOLOGIZE FOR BEING POLITICAL

- "You know I am not much of a politician"—before saying something politically astute
- "I am at a loss what to surmise"—before going on to surmise something smart
- claimed to be sorry for "expressing her opinions always imperfectly understood"—before giving a wise opinion
- in public agreed with those who looked down on "petticoat politicians," referring to an item of underwear as a way of mocking the idea of a woman politician
- once told her sister "Politics is the business of men. I don't care what offices they hold. . . . I care only about *people.*"

★   ★   ★

In all, Dolley spent sixteen years of her life building up Washington, DC, doing more than just about anyone to establish it as a great capital city worthy of a great new country. As the couple prepared to head back to Montpelier, people were sorry to see her go.

She stayed busy, of course. She helped James shape his papers for publication and entertained constant visitors, begging to be informed of the latest news. She started writing light verse about patriotic topics and classical subjects like Greek myths.

She was a world-class aunt to James's thirty nieces and nephews. But as a mom she'd been too permissive, *too* supportive, and her son continually disappointed her with gambling debts, which she always paid.

When James died, she mourned him and the end of their happy forty-one-year marriage. Then she moved back to Washington to be where the action was.

For half a century she was the most important woman on Washington's social scene, someone who knew all twelve of the first presidents. Every First Lady after her sought her advice, and she was awarded one honor after another, like an honorary seat in Congress. When she died at age eighty-one after a stroke, Washington held the largest funeral up until that time.

Like Martha and Abigail before her, Dolley was keenly aware of her place in history, but with her drive she did even more than each of them. Ahead of her time, she opened the doors to women taking a place on the national stage.

CHAPTER 5

Illness, Heroic Journeys, and Texas

Elizabeth Monroe

Louisa Adams

Anna Harrison

Letitia Tyler

Julia Tyler

Elizabeth Monroe (served from 1817–1825)

With the next First Ladies, we segue into a new age—and one not necessarily a step forward for women. It was named the Victorian Era for Queen Victoria, who ruled Great Britain from 1837 to 1901. The British laced themselves up tight, and many Americans did too. It was okay, even fashionable, for women to be invalids, weak, even invisible.

Expectations for First Ladies at this time, unfortunately, were lowered.

Poor Elizabeth Monroe (1768–1830), for example. She had the bad luck to follow the effervescent Dolley. Compared to Dolley, Elizabeth made little impression, or even a bad one.

She married James Monroe at seventeen, and we know little about her before then. She was said to be his partner in everything he did as he went from promising lawyer to political leader, serving his country for forty years. But we'll never be sure of her role—James later stupidly burned all her extensive correspondence.

NO PRESSURES

Another reason for the lackluster nature of some of the First Ladies following Martha, Abigail, and Dolley is that the country was, for the time being, no longer in crisis mode. With the triumphant end of the War of 1812, the country was unified as never before and given a chance to prosper and grow. First Ladies, for the moment, didn't have to rise to a dire occasion. Elizabeth presided over a time of relative peace and quiet—known as the Era of Good Feelings, in fact—that permitted her to be quiet as well.

We know that as First Lady, Elizabeth stole her recipe for oyster loaves directly from Martha Washington and was good friends with Dolley Madison. But Elizabeth lacked their flair and their popularity. For one thing, she was in love with all things French—language, furniture, fashion. To many here, she seemed not American enough, even snobbish, and way too regal. Even the unveiling of the rebuilt White House—now freshly painted white—failed to improve her reputation: people judged her taste in decor too French.

Her only famous deed had in fact taken place in France, when James had served as minister. This was her happiest time. During the French Revolution, in 1794, she played a crucial role in saving the wife of the Marquis de Lafayette—our ally during the American Revolutionary War—from certain execution.

She very likely had opinions about her husband's signature move, the Monroe Doctrine. Impacting America for the next century, Monroe's foreign policy instructed that any attempt by European countries to establish colonies in North or South America would be considered an act of war. Presumably Elizabeth approved of this separation of the Old World and the New World, but we have no record of it.

In her eight White House years, she turned away those not properly dressed, and was often a no-show at her own parties. She claimed illness—possibly arthritis or epilepsy (once she fell into a fireplace)—or else just preferred hanging out with her daughters and grandchildren. Some people disliked her so much they boycotted her events.

After the couple retired to their Virginia plantation, she became nearly invisible and died four years later at the age of sixty-two.

Louisa Adams (served from 1825–1829)

Was there ever a more miserable First Lady than Louisa Adams (1775–1852)?

Her husband, John Quincy Adams, was even more prickly than his father. Despite the stellar example set by his mother, Abigail Adams, he believed that women were inferior. Before their wedding he gave Louisa a reading list to improve her mind, though she was already well educated. She'd been to a convent-run boarding school, where she sang, played harp and piano, wrote poetry— something of a prodigy with no place in society.

Their marriage was strained. They ate silently at meals, each reading his or her own book. If he spoke, it was usually to give her orders. When he saw her wearing makeup, he would set her on his knee and wipe her face clean. While he worked his way up the political ladder, she suffered through multiple miscarriages—nine altogether, plus four pregnancies—fevers, fainting spells, and bouts of depression.

She was a worldly First Lady. Her father had been minister to England, where she was born, and she'd also lived in France and spoke fluent French. As the only First Lady born outside the United States, she couldn't count on the support of her mother-in-law—Abigail never quite trusted her as a "foreigner."

The two women's relationship didn't improve when Louisa accompanied John Q. on an eight-year post as minister to Russia. He insisted that they leave their two oldest sons behind for Abigail to raise.

Louisa was popular at the Russian court—she knew how to behave with the style and grace of a diplomat's wife. But then John was called away to London to negotiate the peace treaty that ended the War of 1812. He summoned her to join him, and in what was one of the most harrowing experiences for any First Lady, Louisa did. It was a forty-day journey by carriage with her seven-year-old son across war-ravaged Europe in the middle of winter. Threats included wolves, untrustworthy servants, hostile mobs, and roving bands of robbers. Filled with "unspeakable terrors" for her son, she took to displaying his toy sword in the window as a warning.

John treated her with more respect after this trip, and she went on to help him campaign for president.

LOUISA AS A WRITER

Passionate about ending slavery and promoting equality for women, Louisa exchanged fervent letters with Angelina and Sarah Grimké, early feminists and abolitionists. An excellent writer, Louisa wrote up her forty-day travel nightmare and published it specifically to destroy a myth—"the fancied weakness of feminine imbecility." She was a writer with low self-esteem; when she wrote her memoirs, she called them *Adventures of a Nobody*.

Once she and John were in the White House, Louisa called it "a dull and stately prison." Abigail had died by then, so no pep talks were forthcoming from her mother-in-law. More irritable than ever, John was obsessed with his work—trying to improve the American economy, opposing slavery, and carrying out the Monroe Doctrine while maintaining peaceful relations with American Indians.

Louisa often kept to her bedroom, unknowingly inhaling poisonous fumes from heaters that burned coal.

It wasn't all gloomy though. She liked her quiet evenings, eating chocolate, reading, composing music and poetry, and playing her harp. She also raised hundreds of silkworms and made silk from their cocoons. But her overall feeling on life as a First Lady remained negative: "There is something in this great unsocial house which depresses me beyond expression."

Women Break Through

1833 Lucretia Mott founds the Female Anti-Slavery Society after she finds out that the new American Anti-Slavery Society is for men only.

After leaving office, John went on to serve seventeen more years in Congress, while Louisa kept working on her antislavery and women's rights causes. Her two oldest sons died suddenly, but she and John seemed to grow closer as they aged. A stroke at the age of seventy-four increased her depression, but she lingered on for three years until she died from a heart attack at age seventy-seven.

Anna Harrison (served in 1841)

Anna Harrison (1775–1864) has the distinction of being the only First Lady who never got to step foot in the White House.

She'd been a fancy young lady from the East Coast, and the first with a formal public education, completing it at a boarding school in New York City. Life after her marriage to William Henry Harrison—an army leader considered heroic for battling American Indians for their land, who later became governor of the Indiana Territory—was harsh. She dutifully followed him from post to post, mostly on the wild new frontier. She had few creature comforts and was constantly under the threat of Indian attack. She single-handedly raised and homeschooled their ten children, and she taught the neighbors' children as well.

Anna looked forward to William's retirement, when they would move to the Ohio farm they owned and they could spend their last years quietly together. But he wasn't quite ready yet and started running for office. Suddenly, at age sixty-eight, he won a landslide victory in the presidential election. When Anna found out, she burst into tears.

With great reluctance, she set about following him to Washington. But on Inauguration Day he gave the longest inauguration speech in American history, got a cold, and died of pneumonia. His one-month term was the shortest of any president, and Anna became the first First Lady to be widowed while holding the title.

Besides outliving William, Anna outlived nine of her ten children. She carried on until age eighty-eight. She was a good grandmother to as many as forty-eight grandkids, including future president Benjamin

Harrison, making her the only First Lady to be both a wife and a grandmother of a president.

WOMEN BREAK THROUGH

1837 Oberlin College admits four women, making it the first coeducational college in America. In between classes, the women are required to serve the men at meals, clean their rooms, and wash their clothes.

1839 Mississippi passes the first law in America that allows wives the right to own property and income (including their own) in their own names. Other states gradually follow.

Letitia Tyler (served from 1841–1842)

John Tyler had two First Ladies during his one term in the White House. First up was Letitia (1790–1842), who knew all the skills of managing a plantation and raising children—she had seven of them in her charge. Overwhelmed with responsibilities in her private life, she desperately wanted John to stay out of public life. She didn't get her way. From the Virginia state legislature he went on to become William Henry Harrison's vice president. And with Harrison's sudden death, he became president.

Two years earlier, when she was just forty-nine, Letitia had suffered a stroke and never fully recovered.

In a wheelchair at a time when the White House had no wheelchair access, she truly was a prisoner in the house. She rested in bed, while telling others how to run things. She avoided any political talk—for example, whether or not she agreed with John's passionate proslavery stance. She tried to be kind to them, but she couldn't imagine living without their thirty slaves.

Women Break Through

1843 Sojourner Truth starts speaking out for women suffrage and against slavery.

Letitia appeared so rarely in public that some wondered whether she even existed. She suffered a second stroke and died at the age of fifty-one, the youngest First Lady to pass away and the first First Lady to die while still holding the title.

Julia Tyler (served from 1844–1845)

John's remarriage less than two years after Letitia's death raised many eyebrows. Plus his new wife, Julia Tyler (1820–1889), was thirty years younger than him.

Julia soon won most people over, though. Part of a prominent New York family, she had made her debut in society at fifteen. She did a bit of modeling for department stores, becoming famous as the "Rose of Long Island." Before she could model much more—considered a scandalous profession for a woman at the time—her father hustled her off on a European tour that opened the world to her. At twenty-four, she had her pick of suitors . . . so why not the president of the United States? Some of his children were older than she was and would resent her for years afterward. But that didn't stop her.

First Lady for eight months, Julia relished the spotlight—unlike most First Ladies of her era. At parties bubbly with champagne, she welcomed guests wearing a tiara, and was attended by twelve maids of honor dressed in white. A great dancer, she introduced the polka. A book called *The Julia Waltzes* was published so that others could learn her favorite songs and dance to them.

"Nothing appears to delight the president more than . . . to hear people sing my praises," she burbled.

Whenever possible she tried to get involved in politics and use her influence, much to the disapproval of male officials.

Julia also had seven children, and after her time in the White House was mistress of Sherwood Forest, their plantation in Virginia. Though she was born a Yankee, she championed the proslavery views of her husband. She believed that slaves had better lives under white rule, denounced *Uncle Tom's Cabin* when it was published in

1852, campaigned against Abraham Lincoln when he ran for reelection in 1864, and was appalled when her home was turned into a school for black children after the Civil War.

Until she died at sixty-nine, she always called herself Mrs. Ex-presidentress.

* * * * * * * * * * * * * * *

JULIA AND TEXAS

One of the biggest controversies at the time was whether or not to make Texas—which at that time was its own country—our next state. Many didn't want another southern, proslavery state to join the United States. But John Tyler was big on expansion, and Julia personally lobbied congressmen on his behalf. She wanted Texas, she got it, and when John signed the 1845 bill officially annexing it, he gave her the gold signing pen. She wore it afterward as a necklace symbolizing her triumph.

* * * * * * * * * * * * * * *

CHAPTER 6

Ambition versus Invisibility

Sarah Polk

Margaret Taylor

Abigail Fillmore

Jane Pierce

Sarah Polk (served from 1845–1849)

With our next four First Ladies, stirrings of ambition—even holding a job after marriage—competed with the repressive Victorian mood that lingered on in the country.

To all appearances, Sarah Polk (1803–1891) was a proper Victorian lady. Secretly she was ambitious—she dared to believe it was her destiny to help in running the country. In another era she might have become a politician herself—for now she could only marry one. She accepted James Polk's proposal on one condition—that he move up from clerking in the Tennessee legislature to running for his own seat in it. He won, and the marriage was on, with her pushing him up the political ladder.

Sarah was wealthy, very well educated, extremely religious, and took the work of her slaves for granted, believing that all people were not created equal.

In the White House, her claim to fame was her lack of fun. She refused to go to horse races or the theater, and she had a reputation for banning dancing, card playing, and alcohol. The Polks never took a vacation and had no children to lighten things up or distract them from their work.

But it wasn't all true. And there was more to her than she showed the public. For one thing, a Washington wife recorded at least one Polk dinner with glasses for six different wines, from pink champagne to ruby port, that "formed a rainbow around each plate."

And Sarah probably had more direct influence on a president than any First Lady since Abigail Adams. Behind the scenes, she ran James's campaigns and had done much to get him elected. He didn't like to read the newspapers but would hand them over and point to the articles he wanted *her* to read. She helped him with his speeches and wasn't afraid to disagree with him—sometimes even in public.

AMERICA EXPANDS

Both Sarah and James were big believers in Manifest Destiny—the idea that Americans were *destined* to settle the entire continent, from the Atlantic to the Pacific. James went to war with Mexico to keep Texas under American control and then to acquire California. He kept on, pressuring Great Britain to resolve the dispute over the Oregon Territory border, thereby adding three more states and parts of two more. Under the Polks, the continent was indeed settled.

Sarah made a point of staying out of the kitchen and preferred the company of men to women. She fired some of the staff and brought in her own unpaid slaves to replace them. She ordered an especially pompous rendition of "Hail to the Chief" to be played whenever her husband entered a room—suspecting that otherwise no one would notice him.

WOMEN BREAK THROUGH

1848 The women's rights movement is sparked at a convention in Seneca Falls, New York, with three hundred delegates led by Elizabeth Cady Stanton and Lucretia Mott. Delegates issue a Declaration of Sentiments calling for equality with men and demanding the right to vote.

1848 New York State passes the Married Women's Property Act, allowing divorced women to keep some of their possessions.

1849 Elizabeth Blackwell is the first woman to graduate from medical school in the United States.

James lived only three months after leaving office. Sarah lived on another forty-two years, wearing black and seldom leaving her home in Nashville. She gained respect during the Civil War by meeting with leaders of both Northern and Southern armies. Her home, Polk Place, was considered neutral ground. After the longest widowhood of any former First Lady, she died at age eighty-seven.

Margaret Taylor (served from 1849–1850)

Margaret Taylor (1788–1852) really, really did not want to be First Lady. Her husband, Zachary Taylor, was a hero of the Mexican-American War (1846–1848), and Margaret was a military wife, following him to one remote military base after another. What with the constant travel, bleak frontier life (she learned how to use a gun), and bearing six children (losing two of them as babies), her health grew delicate.

Even though he wasn't particularly political, Zachary couldn't say no when he was asked to run for president. The very idea of her husband being nominated was to Margaret "a plan to deprive me of his society and shorten his life." She prayed every night for his defeat. All she wanted was to retire with him and have peace and quiet at their Louisiana home. But it was not to be.

During her sixteen months in the White House, Margaret visited with friends and family in her upstairs sitting room, headed up the family table at meals, and went to church every day. But she declined to appear at formal functions. There are no confirmed photos or paintings of her. Her invisibility sparked rumors that she was a backwoods recluse who smoked a crude corncob pipe and had to be locked in the attic—none of which was true.

It was finally starting to become objectionable to have slaves in the White House. The Taylors brought fifteen of their hundred slaves with them, some of them children, but kept them out of the public eye.

Zachary died suddenly while in office, from a stomach upset after eating cherries with iced milk. Margaret had to be torn from his body and never recovered. She died two years later at sixty-three.

Abigail Fillmore (served from 1850–1853)

One of our most bookish First Ladies, Abigail Fillmore (1798–1853) worked for a living. She became a teacher at sixteen, and five years later, Millard Fillmore was one of her prize pupils. He fell in love with her as she introduced him to literature and history, shaping him into lawyer material.

She didn't stop teaching after they were married and became the first First Lady to have held a job after marriage. She did eventually quit to raise her two children. She learned the ways of society as the wife of a congressman and then a vice president who abruptly became president upon Zachary Taylor's death.

During her time as First Lady, Abigail delegated as many of her social duties as she could to her daughter. An old ankle injury (she had twisted it and kept walking on it for days afterward) made their Friday-evening receptions torture for her—two hours of standing and greeting the public.

She believed women had no business speaking in public. Though, in private, Millard rarely made a decision without consulting her first, he didn't always take her advice. At a time when the North and South were edging closer to Civil War, neither of them did anything to fight slavery.

Abigail put most of her energy into music—with three pianos (she taught herself to play), a harp, and guitar. And above all, she loved books. She was such a big reader that Millard turned the Oval Room into a library, while she lobbied Congress for funds to stock it. She spent contented days selecting and arranging books— Shakespeare, history, geography.

WOMEN BREAK THROUGH

1850   Harriet Tubman begins work as a conductor on the Underground Railroad, leading slaves to freedom.

1852   Harriet Beecher Stowe publishes *Uncle Tom's Cabin*, selling three hundred thousand copies that year, changing countless white minds about slavery.

1852   Antioch College becomes the first to admit women (white or black) on an absolutely equal basis, without their having to do the cooking and cleaning.

Abigail didn't even try to hide her relief when Millard lost his bid for reelection. She caught a cold while attending the chilly inauguration ceremony for his successor and developed pneumonia. She died at fifty-five, only twenty-six days after leaving the White House, the shortest life after the White House of any First Lady.

By that time she'd amassed an astounding four thousand books, which for the time was an enormous collection. It was the beginning of the official White House library and the accomplishment for which Abigail is best known.

Jane Pierce (served from 1853–1857)

Few who lived in the White House were as depressed as Jane Pierce (1806–1863).

She was apparently well educated, though she would have received all her education at home. She was so good at the piano that she was encouraged to pursue it professionally. With no self-confidence and a flurry of anxiety symptoms, she turned to books and religion for comfort.

She met handsome Franklin Pierce when they were both students, and he romantically rescued her from a thunderstorm as she fled a library to try to get home. She was twenty-eight when they married—a late age in an era of early marriages. She tried her best to discourage his interest in politics, believing it sinful (and for him it did seem to involve a lot of parties with a lot of wine): "Oh, how I wish he was out of political life!"

Ultimately, he broke his promise to her to leave politics. When she found out he'd gone from Mexican-American War hero to being nominated for president, she fainted. She got her eleven-year-old son Benny to pray with her that Franklin would lose the election.

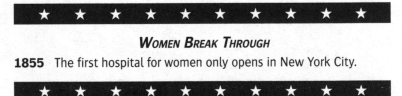

WOMEN BREAK THROUGH

1855 The first hospital for women only opens in New York City.

Jane, always frail, never recovered from the deaths of her three sons. The first had died just days after his birth, the second from typhus at the age of four, nine years before Franklin was elected. The third—beloved Benny— died during a freak train accident just before Franklin's inauguration and both parents had the misfortune to witness it. Jane collapsed, sure that God was punishing her family for its involvement in politics.

She skipped the inauguration, and during his term became known as the "shadow of the White House." She weighed eighty-five pounds, dwindling away with grief, and she stayed mostly out of the public eye.

She did have opinions—she was much more anti-slavery than Franklin was and tried to influence his stance, but with little effect. He believed that the movement to abolish slavery was the greatest threat to America and, in fact, his actions made a Civil War increasingly likely.

JANE THE DISAPPOINTMENT

In a 2014 poll of historians, Jane was voted the most disappointing First Lady, being passive, reluctant, and weak. She was followed by Eliza Johnson, Letitia Tyler, Florence Harding, and Margaret Taylor.

Jane asked friends and family to stand in for her at formal events. Meanwhile, she secluded herself on the second floor, enduring various ailments and writing heartbreaking letters to Benny, begging for his forgiveness.

After retirement, the Pierces traveled abroad, hoping to improve Jane's health. She carried Benny's Bible throughout the journey. But nothing worked, and she sank lower and lower, eventually dying, probably of tuberculosis, as a fifty-seven-year-old recluse.

CHAPTER 7

Civil War Breaks Out

Mary Lincoln

Mary Lincoln (served from 1861–1865)

Probably no First Lady loved the theater more than Mary Lincoln (1818–1882)—and she was a drama queen herself. "The very creature of excitement," said someone who knew her in her twenties.

Her wealthy family had founded her hometown, Lexington, Kentucky, and Mary always had a sense of destiny. Her father wanted her to get a substantial education—not to get a job but to attract the best mate. "If you do not study now," as one Kentucky father said, "after your marriage your mind will collapse and you will fail to amuse your husband." She excelled at school and studied a much wider range of subjects than girls (or boys) usually did at that time.

At eleven she was already sharing political opinions—she was fervently against slavery—and even talking about her plan to marry a president. The only career path open to her was to become a teacher, and she did teach briefly at her old academy. But to get away from a stepmother she loathed, she moved to Springfield, Illinois, to live with her sister, whose husband's family was active in local politics.

Suitors flocked, but Mary was critical, deeming them "uninteresting" and sometimes laughing at them to their faces. Waxing witty and quoting Shakespeare and other poets, she would debate with the men—often winning and jolting their egos. Most men were afraid of her.

★ ★ ★ ★ ★ ★ ★ ★ ★ ★ ★ ★ ★ ★ ★

MARY AND MARRIAGE

Mary didn't fret about men failing to propose marriage—she enjoyed her freedom. She had noticed that women lost some of it after the "crime of matrimony" and wanted to marry for love. "Why is it that married folks always become so serious?" she wrote a friend.

★ ★ ★ ★ ★ ★ ★ ★ ★ ★ ★ ★ ★ ★ ★

A gangly young lawyer named Abraham Lincoln wasn't afraid of her, but his awkwardness around women wasn't appealing. "Oh, boys," he said upon entering a Springfield gathering, "how clean these girls look!"

Mary softened his rough edges, and he laughed at her wit. After an on-again, off-again engagement (he didn't see how he could support her in the style she was accustomed to, and neither did her family), they married. Their first home was a room at a boardinghouse called the Globe Tavern. It was the nicest place he'd ever lived—and the worst she'd ever seen.

But they were devoted to each other. At his next birthday she gave a speech that ended with, "I am so glad you have a birthday. I feel so grateful to your mother."

While Abraham traveled and became more established in his career, Mary was a housewife, caring for their four sons. She set about making her home a theater of domestic bliss. To master the necessary skills, she subscribed to *Godey's Lady's Book,* a popular new magazine for women, and took its message to heart: "The perfection of womanhood is the wife and mother . . . the woman is truly the light of the home."

Mary positively adored her sons, and her philosophy of child-rearing was basically to let the boys have a good time.

But in a very rare role for a woman of her time, she also became Abraham's main adviser as his political career took off. She was highly ambitious for them both. His other, male advisers grumbled over her involvement, but she was in her element: "I've become quite a politician," she crowed, admitting the unladylike nature of her role.

She was the one who got him to turn down the governorship of Oregon—because it seemed like a dead end to her. She thought it a much better path for him to campaign for Congress, which he did. When he accepted the nomination to become senator, Mary was the only one of his advisers who told him to go ahead with the "house divided against itself cannot stand" speech. "It will make you president," she insisted, and the speech put him on the map.

★ ★ ★ ★ ★ ★ ★ ★ ★ ★ ★ ★ ★ ★ ★

THINGS MARY DID
- made almost all the family's clothes and laundered them
- hauled wood
- gardened
- made her own cheese and ice cream
- preserved fruit
- cleaned (carrying the water in from a pump outside)
- milked the cow
- constantly killed insects—every night she set out dishes of a potion to kill cockroaches, and every morning she dumped the mess outside
- and much more

★ ★ ★ ★ ★ ★ ★ ★ ★ ★ ★ ★ ★ ★ ★

She guided him during his presidential campaign, and he was proud of her: "Here I am, and here is Mrs. Lincoln. And that's the long and short of it," he would say by way of a joke about their sixteen-inch difference in height.

As their White House years began, she wrote, "Washington is perfectly charming. . . . I am beginning to feel so perfectly at home and enjoy everything so much. Every evening our blue room is filled with the elite of the land."

Wanting to make her new home a gathering place for intellectuals, she formed a group that met to discuss books, current events, and gossip, while he worked upstairs. He discouraged the group because he didn't trust them not to reveal presidential secrets, but they met for the rest of the Lincolns' White House years.

WOMEN BREAK THROUGH

1861 The first women's college opens, Vassar Female College, in Poughkeepsie, New York. A wealthy brewer named Matthew Vassar founded it, having been inspired by his niece, a well-educated woman who believed that higher learning would help women be better mothers.

At a time when women weren't even supposed to know the difference between the political parties, Mary kept on advising her husband. She would phrase her ideas apologetically: "I have a great terror of *strong*-minded ladies," she would say before giving her strong opinions. But he was assembling a whole cabinet of men to assist him, and he stopped taking her advice. "If I listened to you, I should soon be without a cabinet," he said, and all the men around him loudly agreed.

Now that they'd reached the White House, unfortunately, Mary began losing her privileged partnership role. The cataclysmic Civil War (1861–1865) broke out as soon as he was elected. Abraham was intent on keeping the United States together, while the Southern states were determined to break away, detesting his support for banning slavery. He assumed greater and greater responsibilities as commander in chief of the Northern troops, and the war subsumed him, taking him away from her.

Mary cast about for a way to channel her energy and found it in refurbishing the White House, which had grown embarrassingly shabby. She saw its potential to be the grandest theater in the land and was delighted when Congress gave her a budget. Her expectations exceeded her budget, though, and she was soon in hot water for her extravagances.

BEHIND ABRAHAM'S BACK

Not all of Mary's moves were ethical, and she had to keep some from Abraham, who had the strictest of moral codes. She fought for jobs for her relatives, something other men did but he wouldn't have done. In exchange for their votes, during a campaign, behind his back she cultivated several dozen politicians he considered unscrupulous. She figured out creative ways to pad budgets around the White House to cover her expenses in refurbishing it. One of her least popular attempts to repay the debt was to ask for a salary for herself for running the kitchen. A woman earning a salary? No one took it seriously.

By then Mary was a target of abuse no matter what she did in her role. The North criticized her for being too southern, the South criticized her for being a traitor. She courted controversy—her best friend, who was also her dressmaker, was an ex-slave who had bought her freedom. And Mary was the first First Lady to invite blacks into the White House as guests. Her hatred of slavery had never wavered, and she was almost certainly a factor in Abraham's highly controversial Emancipation

Proclamation, banning slavery in ten states. The proclamation made him more hated than ever in the South, and death threats against him multiplied.

* * * * * * * * * * * * * *

MARY AND THE RIGHT TO VOTE

Women's suffrage was starting to be a hot topic. Like most people of her day, Mary considered voting to be unwomanly. But perhaps because of her, Abraham was the first major politician to suggest extending the right to vote to women. Twelve years before the first women's rights convention, he made a statement supporting "female suffrage." Though Mary disagreed, she backed the establishment of a female nursing corps and helped women get jobs in the Treasury and War departments.

* * * * * * * * * * * * * *

Sometimes, Mary was her own worst enemy. Whenever she was crossed, her attitude was "Don't you know who I am?" which rubbed possible allies the wrong way.

Many frowned at the way she let her sons run wild. They were allowed to spray important people with fire hoses, break mirrors, burst into cabinet meetings, and lock doors, and they had an insane amount of pets.

Mary had been traumatized earlier when one of her sons had died as a baby, and when eleven-year-old Willy died in the White House, she went into a deep depression. She held at least eight séances trying to communicate with his spirit. Her grief was such that Abraham warned she would have to be sent to a mental hospital if she couldn't control it.

Mary pulled herself together to become active in the war effort, providing care to soldiers, and she visited troops with Abraham. She poured energy into an organization that helped recently freed slaves who had nowhere to go.

She also worked hard to keep Abraham's spirits up during the exhausting and trying war years. She got him to attend plays with her. On the night he was shot and killed—becoming the first president to be assassinated—they were watching a comedy and she was holding his hand.

Mary never recovered from the shock. "All is over with me," she said again and again. "I have almost become blind with weeping."

During her last seventeen years, she lived in France and Germany for long periods of time, and was heavily dependent on her teenage son Tad. When he died, she slipped further into despair.

★ ★ ★ ★ ★ ★ ★ ★ ★ ★ ★ ★ ★

WHAT'S UP WITH THE LINCOLN BEDROOM?

The Lincoln Bedroom, decorated in elegant Victorian style, is the only room in the White House dedicated to a single president. Today, special friends of the First Couple are sometimes treated with an overnight stay there. It wasn't actually where the Lincolns slept. It was used as Abraham's personal office. All the furniture in it has some connection to Mary, Abraham, or Willy, and it's considered a special, sacred place—with ghosts, some say.

★ ★ ★ ★ ★ ★ ★ ★ ★ ★ ★ ★ ★

She was still close to Robert, her remaining son, and was anxious to advise him as he entered politics. But as her behavior became eccentric and embarrassing in polite society, he had her judged insane and committed to a mental hospital. Though she was able to free herself within four months, she refused to forgive him until shortly before she died.

She called Robert a "monster of mankind." But when there were rumors he might be running for president, she gleefully fantasized about who he should pick for his cabinet....

MARY'S MIND

Mary was definitely moody and theatrical. But whole books have been published on what, if any, mental problems she may have had:

- She may have suffered from depression, compounded by the tragedies she endured and her restricted life as a well-educated woman.
- Her compulsive shopping while in the White House and afterward led some to think she had a bipolar disorder.
- Toward the end of the war, she suffered a serious head injury in a carriage accident, leading some to suspect brain damage.
- Her direct experience of her beloved husband's death could have led to post-traumatic stress disorder and made her unstable.

Psychology was in its infancy during her lifetime. Mary's "cure" called for rest, fresh air, an orderly day, and music by Chopin and Beethoven. We'll likely never know an accurate medical diagnosis.

Mary died at sixty-three after a stroke. As she had written to a friend during her declining years: "What a world of anguish this is—and how I have been made to suffer!" Such has been the complaint of other First Ladies, but for Mary it was all too true.

CHAPTER 8

And Now the "New Woman Era"

Eliza Johnson

Julia Grant

Lucy Hayes

Lucretia Garfield

Eliza Johnson (served from 1865–1869)

After the shock of Lincoln's assassination, the next couple to move into the White House was ill prepared for their role. "We are plain people from Tennessee," pleaded their daughter, "called here for a little time by the nation's calamity, and I hope too much will not be expected of us." Mary Lincoln was in no condition to offer them help.

Eliza Johnson (1810–1876) had been her husband's teacher. She married at only sixteen, the youngest age of any future First Ladies, and began enhancing eighteen-year-old Andrew Johnson's knowledge right away.

She had received a good basic eighth-grade education and helped support her family by making quilts and sandals. He was an expert tailor (the only president who made his own suits), but had never been to school. She built on what he knew—the alphabet, a little bit of reading—and led him to writing and arithmetic. Her skills in and out of the house had a lot to do with Andrew's success as a politician.

After the Emancipation Proclamation of 1863, the Johnsons freed their slaves, who then stayed on as paid servants.

After the birth of their fifth child, Eliza's health declined. Apparently stricken with tuberculosis, she stayed away from Washington when Andrew was vice president. But when he abruptly became president, she was supposed to join him. She stalled for four months and eventually moved into a second-floor room that she made into the center of activity for her family.

One of our least-known First Ladies, Eliza made only two public appearances as her husband presided over a country in postwar chaos. She spent her time clipping magazine and newspaper articles about Andrew. He would drop by to go over current events with her and get his talking points for his next day. At night she would show him the clippings most favorable to him. Mostly, though, they were negative, and she'd save those for the morning so as not to trouble his sleep.

WOMEN BREAK THROUGH

1868 Publication of *Little Women* by former Civil War nurse Louisa May Alcott. For its portrayal of sisterly camaraderie and of strong, independent heroine Jo March, it is a favorite book of Hillary Clinton, Barbara Bush, Laura Bush, Gloria Steinem, Jane Yolen, and J. K. Rowling, among many others.

It was a blow to Eliza when Andrew's political enemies came up with a way to try to get him removed from office. For "high crimes and misdemeanors" (like firing a cabinet member), he became the first president to be impeached, or brought to trial. Eliza supported him throughout the trial and was relieved that the vote to convict him fell just short of the necessary majority, so he was able to finish his term. Still hated in Washington, they were greeted as heroes when they eventually returned to Tennessee.

In worsening health, Eliza lingered on for seven years afterward, until at sixty-five, she died six months after her husband.

The Clippings of Eliza

Though the Johnsons were from a Southern slave state, Andrew had supported the North during the Civil War. But many in Congress felt that as president he was too quick to bring the Southern states back into the United States, without penalties for them and without protection for former slaves. He opposed the Fourteenth Amendment giving citizenship to African Americans. His leadership was weak during this postwar Reconstruction, as the country tried to unite once again, and much to Eliza's sorrow he grew deeply unpopular.

Julia Grant (served from 1869–1877)

Julia Grant (1826–1902) radiated contentment. She called her childhood "one long summer of sunshine, flowers, and smiles." She went to a fancy boarding school and was a dancer and good horsewoman.

She was equally fond of being an army wife, which began in 1848, when she married Ulysses S. Grant. He fought in the Mexican-American War and reached the height of popularity as the commander of all the Northern armies during the Civil War. While raising four children, she joined her husband at his military posts whenever she could, and called this "the happiest period" of her life. Once Southern troops had finally surrendered to Ulysses, bringing the Civil War to an end, she grew very ambitious for him, envisioning a path straight to what she saw as the finest house in the land—the White House.

Some political wives dislike the spotlight, but Julia was the opposite—the brighter and bigger the spotlight the better. When she reached the White House, she *loved* being First Lady—likening it to "a bright and beautiful dream."

The couple were devoted to each other. With one eye that moved uncontrollably, Julia walked awkwardly if she didn't have someone guiding her. Ulysses talked her out of having corrective surgery—he worshiped her the way she was. She worshiped him back, once telling the queen of England that her husband was "a great ruler" on a par with Her Highness.

She was an active adviser in private, particularly when it came to getting relatives and friends political appointments. In public she was the first First Lady to issue a press release (about fashion trends). She made a point of keeping newspapers informed about her activities and her family's, leading to the long tradition of people wanting to know all about the First Family.

Ulysses was against slavery, while she was from a slaveholding family in Missouri and dependent on it. To his relief, she reluctantly changed her mind after the Emancipation Proclamation and when her personal slave, also named Julia, ran away. With visitors, her stated policy was to "admit all who call," but police at the gates still barred blacks from entering, and she never questioned it. In later life she did fight for women's suffrage.

★ ★ ★ ★ ★ ★ ★ ★ ★ ★

Women Break Through

1869 The territory of Wyoming is the first to grant women the right to vote, followed by Utah in 1870.

1870 Ellen Swallow Richards is the first woman accepted to any school of science and technology (Massachusetts Institute of Technology).

1870 The University of Michigan allows women to enroll.

1870 In Wyoming, for the first time in American history, women are allowed to serve on a grand jury.

1872 Victoria Woodhull is the first woman to run for U.S. president, against Ulysses S. Grant. Hardly anyone takes her campaign seriously, and votes for her aren't counted.

1877 Twenty-three states now allow women to control their own property.

★ ★ ★ ★ ★ ★ ★ ★ ★ ★

Ulysses, though popular, refused to run for a third term, a decision *not* popular with his wife. On the day they left the White House, Julia cried: Why couldn't life in this glamorous house go on forever? He cheered her up by taking her on a trip around the world.

She hated smoking, and whenever she discovered cigars that he had stashed, she threw them out. But he kept on, eventually developing mouth cancer. He quickly wrote up his memoirs so as to leave her a wealthy widow.

She later summed up their life: "The light of his glorious fame still reaches out to me, falls upon me, and warms me."

She died at seventy-six of heart disease.

Lucy Hayes (served from 1877–1881)

As times changed and women advanced, First Ladies became less shadows of their husbands and more accomplished, with feats of their own.

The first one to graduate from college was Lucy Hayes (1831–1889), who became a role model for educated women. Fans hailed her as representing the "new woman era."

She'd been to Wesleyan Female College in Cincinnati, and Rutherford Hayes, a student at Harvard Law School, admired her intellect as well as her beauty and "her low sweet voice." In the first twenty years of their happy marriage Lucy had eight children, of whom five grew into adulthood.

During their White House years, both were deeply interested in American antiques and history. Unlike others before them, they kept careful records of their deeds. They even had the first typewriter in the White House.

Lucy had some strong positions. Deeply religious, she firmly opposed slavery and converted Rutherford to her point of view. Doing what she could to help the country recover from the Civil War, she visited many schools, including colleges for African Americans and for the deaf, advocating education for all. She frequently visited injured vets and helped several keep their positions on the White House staff.

She was an advocate of temperance, the movement to reduce alcohol use, but did not want to be publicly connected with the cause. It was Rutherford who made the unpopular decision to ban alcoholic beverages from the White House, but she fully supported him and was later mocked as "Lemonade Lucy." Instead of serving alcohol, she would take her guests on long strolls through the gardens.

She was the first president of the Women's Home Missionary Society and spoke out about women: "Elevate women and you lift up the home—exalt the home and you lift up the nation."

Still, many felt that, as a beloved woman in a position of power, she could have done more to speed up change.

Women Break Through

1879 After great resistance from state bar associations, Belva Ann Lockwood becomes one of the first female lawyers and later a political activist.

One area where Lucy disappointed was women's rights, even though she believed "Woman's mind is as strong as man's, equal in all things and superior in some." Raised since a young girl to believe that women should be sweet rather than strong, she couldn't quite make the leap past the stereotypes of her day. She refused to support a bill that would allow women lawyers to argue before the Supreme Court. Two of her aunts were vocal supporters of women's right to vote, but she never took a public stand. She believed the very notion improper, deferring to her husband's belief that motherhood and politics were not compatible.

She died at fifty-seven of a stroke.

Lucretia Garfield (served in 1881)

Lucretia Garfield (1832–1918) was another well-educated First Lady. She met James Garfield while they were college classmates; she knew Greek and Latin, and worked as an art teacher before their marriage.

While he served in the army and worked his way up in politics, she had eight children (five survived to adulthood), sometimes referring to them as "young barbarians." One grew up to be a member of Theodore Roosevelt's cabinet, and another became part of Woodrow Wilson's cabinet.

As First Lady, Lucretia was unusually private. She refused to pose for campaign photographs and was bored by her social duties. She much preferred literary salons or cozy dinners with their two teenage sons, discussing what they were studying in school. But she was conscientious and made a point of trying hard, hosting dinners and twice-weekly receptions that everyone enjoyed. She liked wine and lifted the ban on alcohol.

"I really believe that my husband is the right man to lead the country," she said. She never lost faith in James even when confronted with evidence that he was cheating on her. She gave him advice, played a direct role in his appointments, and planned to bring many authors and artists to the White House, envisioning a celebration of culture.

But less than a year into his term, he was shot by a political enemy. She faithfully sat by his bed for the next eighty days. Everything written about him had to be sent to her first for review. Of his team of doctors, one was a woman, and when Lucretia found out the woman was paid half of what the men got, she cried "discrimination" and took action to make sure they were all paid the same.

She became a national heroine for her devotion, and after James died she was awarded a large pension. For another thirty-six years, her life was strictly private, though she stayed active with the Red Cross and preserved her husband's papers.

She died at eighty-five in South Pasadena in a beautiful arts and crafts mansion of her own design.

CHAPTER 9

The Modern Woman Emerges

Frances Cleveland

Caroline Harrison

Ida McKinley

Edith Roosevelt

Helen Taft

Frances Cleveland
(served from 1886–1889 and 1893–1897)

One of our highest-energy First Ladies, Frances Cleveland (1864–1947) first met her future husband when she was a newborn. Yes, there was a twenty-seven-year age difference between them.

As a devoted family friend, Grover Cleveland bought Frances her first baby carriage and later administrated her family's estate. He wasn't Frances's legal guardian, but he guided her education. When she entered Wells College, he kept her room bright with flowers until she graduated. He actually told people he was "waiting for his wife to grow up."

Then America's youngest First Lady married Grover Cleveland—the bachelor president—when she was just twenty-one. This, the first wedding of a president to take place in the White House, made a huge national splash.

FRANCES'S DILEMMA

Frances didn't take issue in public with Grover, who later wrote: "Sensible and responsible women do not want to vote," listing all the reasons why this would go against nature. She showed no direct influence on improving the status of women, though she seemed to lean that way. At her wedding, the traditional "honor, love, and obey" part of her vows was replaced with "honor, love, and keep"—a rare move. Planning her receptions, she insisted on having one on Saturday afternoons, when women with jobs were free to come (Grover disapproved), and she did advocate for women's education.

Frances believed that it was improper for women to speak in public and was never interviewed. But she was a celebrity in the vein of Dolley Madison and one of the most popular women ever to serve as First Lady. Her influence was not so much political as trendsetting. At her lunches she served the latest craze—"chewing gum done up in fancy papers"—for dessert. When newspapers falsely reported that she had given up wearing a bustle—the cumbersome frame enlarging the back of a woman's skirt—women all over America stopped wearing one, too. It was the end of a major trend in Victorian fashion that made it difficult for women to move freely.

All sorts of products (underwear, soap, perfumes) were named for her without her consent. Cosmetics included arsenic (a poison), touted as the reason for her perfect complexion.

WOMEN BREAK THROUGH

1887   The first female American mayor is elected in Argonia, Kansas.
1895   The word "feminist" first appears in print: a woman who "has in her the capacity of fighting her way back to independence."
1896   Women can now vote in four states.

While in the White House, Grover fought corruption and tried to limit the role of government. Meanwhile Frances had three daughters—Ruth, Esther, and Marion—who also became celebrities. (Her two sons were born later.) Once, she looked out the window and saw total strangers passing around baby Ruth (the famous candy bar was named for her daughter). Despite assassination attempts, White House security was not then a priority, and she immediately had the grounds locked to keep the First Children safer.

Grover was bested in the next election by Benjamin Harrison, who ran a stronger campaign, and the Clevelands had to leave the White House for a time. But they returned, with Grover winning his second term largely because of his wife's charisma.

Frances had the distinction of being the twenty-second *and* the twenty-fourth First Lady, the only one to serve nonconsecutive terms.

Later, five years after Grover died, she became the first presidential widow to remarry. She married a professor of archaeology and remained a figure of note in Princeton, New Jersey—working for groups opposed to women's suffrage, urging people to take the threat of World War I seriously and prepare a strong national defense, collecting clothes for the poor during the Great Depression, and taking part in university life. She died at age eighty-three.

Caroline Harrison (served from 1889–1892)

Caroline Harrison (1832–1892) was no Frances Cleveland. She was not as popular, considered a bit bland, and was much more serious. She wanted to make a difference.

She was a college graduate, a talented pianist and painter, and worked as a music teacher until marrying Benjamin Harrison—the grandson of President William Henry Harrison—and considered the best divorce lawyer in Indianapolis. They had much in common politically, including a commitment to enforcing voting rights for newly freed slaves.

During her husband's presidency, Caroline worked for worthy causes and didn't hesitate to support women. Most notably, she helped raise money for the medical school at Johns Hopkins University on the condition that it admit women. And she helped found the Daughters of the American Revolution (DAR), serving as its first president. She hoped this group—for the direct descendants of those who fought for independence during the Revolutionary War—would lobby for women's suffrage, but instead it focused on promoting patriotism and historic conservation.

★   ★   ★

WISE WORDS

She was the first First Lady to deliver a speech in public that she had written: "It has been made plain that much of [this country's] success was due to . . . women of that era. . . . I feel sure that their daughters can perpetuate a society worthy the cause and worthy themselves."

★   ★   ★

She was responsible for the hiring of the first woman employee at the White House, a secretary. Instead of letting anyone take pictures of her two children, she asked one woman to serve as the official photographer.

An expert china painter, she went around and repaired all the china she could find around the house, also giving classes in art and foreign languages. She was deeply interested in the history of the White House. Congress wouldn't allow her much of a budget to modernize it, but she was able to get electricity installed (though she and everyone else were afraid to turn off the light switches for fear of electric shock).

While researching all the boxes in the attic, she made it her mission to get rid of the rats frolicking there. She took a guard with a gun up with her, and whenever a rat popped up she would scream and he would shoot it.

Two pregnancies, a miscarriage, a serious fall, and depression took a toll on Caroline's health. Plus the marriage didn't seem to be close—when Benjamin ran for a second term, she was totally caught by surprise. There were also rumors that he was having an affair with her niece. She fell ill with tuberculosis and took a summer away from Washington to recover.

A few weeks after she returned to the White House, she died at the age of sixty. (Benjamin later married the niece, permanently estranging him from his children.)

Ida McKinley (served from 1897–1901)

In later life, poor Ida McKinley (1847–1907) seemed to age visibly even as you looked at her.

But she wasn't always this way. In her twenties she'd been able to hike ten miles a day. Her education included a fashionable finishing school and a grand tour of Europe. The first First Lady to hold a job other than teaching, she was working as a manager at her father's bank (a job normally held by men) when she went to a picnic and met young lawyer and Civil War hero William McKinley.

Three years after they married, she lost her two young daughters (one died as an infant and the other of typhoid fever) as well as her mother. She never overcame the losses. She began to have fainting spells and what seemed to be epileptic seizures, which at the time were considered a source of embarrassment. William was utterly devoted to his wife and began arranging their life around her needs. But he didn't halt his political career. He continued running for office, trying to include her as much as she was up to.

During their time in the White House, he led the country out of an economic depression and annexed Hawaii. He also won the Spanish-American War, which further expanded America with control over Puerto Rico, Guam, the Philippine Islands, and (temporarily) Cuba. Ida privately gave him advice on his activities and spoke out against his critics.

At public receptions she would be carried into the room, then seated in a blue velvet chair to receive guests, holding a bouquet of flowers to indicate that she didn't want to shake hands. During private dinners she always sat at her husband's side instead of the opposite end of the table. That way, he could keep an eye on her. Whenever she experienced a seizure, he would delicately place a cloth napkin over her face and direct the conversation elsewhere, removing the napkin when she was well again. He became adept at the maneuver and could do various unrelated things with his other hand.

As ghostly as she was, Ida was the first First Lady to publicly support women's right to vote. She also supported the Red Cross and Crittenden House, a shelter for homeless women, and was in favor of more education for women.

But mostly she remained out of the public eye, sitting in a rocking chair and crocheting bedroom slippers. Doctors could do little except keep her sedated. Slippers were more than just a hobby—she made 3,500 pairs of them that were then auctioned for charity. She was obsessed with her lost girls, and her moods made the White House a gloomy place.

Meanwhile, William was scoring points all over the place with his saintly devotion to his invalid wife. Voters admired him for it and elected him to a second term.

After William was assassinated by a political enemy, Ida's seizures stopped, leading some to wonder whether she was just being manipulative the whole time.

But she remained in a deep depression until her death, six years later, at the age of fifty-nine.

Edith Roosevelt (served from 1901–1909)

"One hates to feel that all one's life is public property," said Edith Roosevelt (1861–1948)—but she adapted skillfully to her role.

Another well-educated woman, Edith was an avid reader—"not only cultured but scholarly," said her husband, Theodore Roosevelt (TR).

The two had been friends since childhood. Her name showed up often in his diary, and she visited him at Harvard College. He married someone else, who died three years later, leaving him with a feisty daughter, Alice. When he married Edith, she insisted that Alice live with them, raising her as her own along with their five children.

Edith ran a tight ship, extremely organized in running the household and handling the finances. Besides keeping her large brood happy, she also sort of managed TR, who had extra energy and lived life to the fullest. In fact, she tended to think of TR as the biggest of her children. "Now remember to be good while I'm away," she once told him absentmindedly.

After the shock of William McKinley's assassination, making TR the youngest president, she carried the same skill set into the White House. Their family life remained close and full of fun. She wanted to make the children's lives as normal as possible. This included having innumerable dogs and cats and Alice's pet snake, horseback riding, and so much roughhousing with their father that some wondered if the building could withstand the strain.

★   ★   ★   ★   ★   ★   ★   ★   ★   ★

WOMEN BREAK THROUGH

1902 The first U.S. postage stamp picturing an American woman is issued: Martha Washington.

TR was a leader of the Progressive Era, a time of rooting out corruption, promoting the scientific method and modernization, conservation of natural resources, and expansion. He began construction of the Panama Canal to make access to Latin America easier. Edith was the one who kept TR grounded, giving him lots of advice, reading the newspapers for him, and influencing his appointments. She held a meeting every week of the cabinet wives. A friend called her "the perfection of invisible government."

She was basically forward thinking, but removed those who she considered improper or scandalous, including black women, from White House invitation lists. Despite family ties, she disapproved of Franklin Roosevelt (a cousin) politically and made a public speech in support of one of his opponents.

After they left the White House, she had a series of heartbreaks: one son died in World War I, followed by TR's death, and then two more sons died in World War II. She mourned deeply, but kept moving. She traveled all around the world and enjoyed her surviving children and grandchildren. She never got completely out of politics. She supported any candidate who ran against Franklin, objecting with irritation when anyone tried to compare FDR to TR.

When Edith died at the age of eighty-seven, *Life* magazine called her "one of the strongest-minded and strongest-willed presidential wives who ever lived in the White House."

Helen Taft (served from 1909–1913)

Helen Taft (1861–1943) was quite the modern woman. She smoked cigarettes, drank beer, played cards for money, traveled widely, and found the restrictions on women's roles frustrating.

She went to private schools, specializing in music. She worked as a teacher for a while, and then in her father's law office. She met the "adorable" William Taft, a young lawyer, at a sledding party. He called her a "treasure—self-contained, independent, and of unusual application." Regarding women's roles, William was a man ahead of his time. When speculating whether they would ever reach Washington "in any official capacity," he actually thought they would—when *she* became secretary of the treasury.

Though Helen supported women's suffrage, she couldn't get past the usual convention that women didn't belong in politics—even though in another era, she could have been a woman to run for office. But with women not even having the right to vote, she concentrated on her husband's career while raising their three children. His dream job was justice of the Supreme Court. Helen wanted him to think bigger and encouraged him to shoot for the presidency.

When they entered the White House, she was the most well-traveled First Lady in history. She had been with him every step of the way on his diplomatic missions around the world, which she had encouraged him to take on. She had loved her journeys to Japan, China, and the Philippines.

She was the first First Lady to ride with her husband on Inauguration Day to the White House. "Of course, there was objection, but I had my way," she gloated. It was a small thing, but "I had a secret elation in doing something that no other woman had done."

★   ★   ★

A RARE FIRST LADY STATEMENT
"I love public life," Helen said during William's campaign.

★   ★   ★

Helen planned to turn Washington into a major cultural center and started talking up her ideas with Congress. Unfortunately, only two months after the inauguration, she suffered a stroke. As she recuperated, she ate in the pantry while eavesdropping on her husband's dinner conversations so she wouldn't feel left out.

Her speech never fully recovered, but with hard work and William's strong support, she was back on her job in a year.

She limited her public appearances but was still noticeably involved in his decisions. He even joked that he was her copresident. When he bought the first stamp that advocated votes for women, someone asked what he would do with it and he said, "I'll put it on a letter to Mrs. Taft!"

She brought East Asian touches to the White House, with tapestries, screens, and palm plants. Most famously, she planted two Japanese cherry trees, inaugurating the city's stunning cherry tree celebration held every spring.

She not only welcomed blacks at events but also divorced people (divorce still being considered disgraceful), and supported new immigrants at a time when most feared they were ruining the country.

Upon leaving the White House, William continued his distinguished career. He went on to be appointed Chief Justice of the Supreme Court, his heart's desire, making Helen the only woman to be First Lady and wife of a justice. Her new role wasn't nearly as demanding as First Lady, and she lived quietly, encouraging her two sons to enter politics and her daughter to study for a doctorate degree. She died at eighty-one, having outlived William by thirteen years.

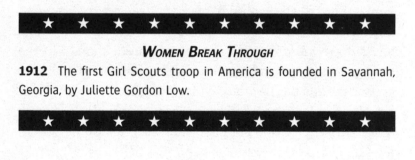

WOMEN BREAK THROUGH

1912 The first Girl Scouts troop in America is founded in Savannah, Georgia, by Juliette Gordon Low.

CHAPTER 10

The Artist and the First Woman Prez

Ellen Wilson

Edith Wilson

Ellen Wilson (served from 1913–1914)

During Woodrow Wilson's two terms, he had two wives. Each woman's name began with "E" and each was influential, though in different ways.

Ellen Wilson (1860–1914) was the first First Lady to earn money on her own—not from anything to do with politics but from art. A talented painter, she had supported herself by painting portraits.

Woodrow Wilson first saw Ellen when she was a baby and he was six years older. Later, when they met again, he was definitely attracted: "What splendid laughing eyes!"

Ellen was a free spirit, mastering her craft, not too interested in marriage, and so picky about a mate that she was known as "Ellie, the Man Hater." Her goal was to use the money from her painting to finance a boardinghouse for women. While going to art school in New York, she took full advantage of the city's galleries, theaters, and lectures. Woodrow was appalled when she sometimes attended events without a male escort.

WOMEN BREAK THROUGH

1913 Five thousand suffragettes march down Pennsylvania Avenue in Washington to make their point and rally for support. Men gather to spit at them, slap, and poke them with lighted cigars.

1914 Margaret Sanger introduces the term "birth control" in her magazine, going on to be a pioneer in making it available, for which she is imprisoned several times.

He felt guilty when she gave up a promising career to marry him. But she was soon wrapped up in life as the mother of their three daughters and as a full-time aide to him as a distinguished professor of political science at Princeton University.

"I am naturally the most unambitious of women," Ellen once said, "and life in the White House has no attractions for me." And yet, once the Wilsons reached it, she saw in her role an opportunity to do good. While Woodrow busied himself with becoming another strong leader of the Progressive Era, Ellen had her own agenda. It included ending child labor and improving working conditions. She even campaigned for women to finally get their own bathrooms in government offices.

She was clearly intrigued by women's suffrage, but Woodrow was opposed to it then, so she didn't take a public stand. She waffled on the issue, wondering if maybe the right to vote should be reserved for women who worked outside the home.

Behind the scenes, she was Woodrow's biggest supporter, helping with speeches, advising him on his advisers. "You see what a wise wife I have!" Woodrow told a friend. Unusually easygoing, she was even tolerant of his mistress.

Ellen still found time for her painting and had a studio with a skylight installed at the White House. Planning weddings for her daughters interfered—"Three daughters take more time than three canvases." But she exhibited her work and even sold paintings—the first sale of art ever by a First Lady—donating the money to poor children in the South. And while the art world was notoriously prejudiced against women—the *New York Times* patronized her White House paintings as "the honest student work of an amateur"—she may have encouraged other artistic women to take risks.

★ ★ ★ ★ ★ ★ ★ ★ ★ ★ ★ ★ ★ ★

HOW ELLEN'S CAUSE LED TO ELEANOR'S

Ellen was the first First Lady to really pick a cause of her own (not her husband's): improving conditions in Washington slums. One-fifth of the city's black population lived in wretched conditions in rundown alleys between the main streets, and she was the first government official to pay attention. She helped draft the Alley Bill for Congress and took congressmen on personal tours so they could see for themselves. This was a symbolic step for someone who was the descendant of slave owners.

During her last illness, she let it be known that it would ease her death if the Alley Bill was passed—and Congress passed it. As World War I broke out, the issue got buried. Critics mocked her efforts as comic. But they were later of great inspiration to Eleanor Roosevelt, whose first bill picked up Ellen's idea to clean up the Washington slums and who went on to become one of our great reformers.

★ ★ ★ ★ ★ ★ ★ ★ ★ ★ ★ ★ ★ ★

Ellen struggled with chronic kidney problems and also with depression. After a fall in her bedroom she never recovered, fading away for five months. When World War I broke out in Europe, Woodrow found it difficult to turn his attention from her to the crisis. She died at fifty-four, having served as First Lady for only seventeen months.

On the day before her death, she made her doctor promise to tell Woodrow that she hoped he would marry again.

And Woodrow obeyed.

Edith Wilson (served from 1915–1921)

Fifteen months later, Woodrow married Edith Galt (1872–1961), a member of the Virginia aristocracy.

Edith had been mostly homeschooled by her grandmother, with little formal education beyond a few semesters in music at a girls' finishing school.

For twelve years she was married to a wealthy jeweler in Washington. She had one son who died a few days after his birth and after that was unable to have more children. When her husband died suddenly, Edith shrewdly hired a manager who kept the jewelry firm running smoothly.

Edith knew nothing about politics—she didn't even know who the candidates were in Woodrow's first election. When she met the mourning president through mutual friends, it was said to be the first time he had laughed since Ellen's death.

★ ★ ★ ★ ★ ★ ★ ★ ★ ★

WOMEN BREAK THROUGH

1916 Jeannette Rankin of Montana is the first woman elected to Congress. (By 2015, there are 108 women in Congress.)

1917 Alice Paul and her National Woman's Party picket the White House to keep up the pressure on Wilson to support women's suffrage. When Paul is imprisoned she goes on a hunger strike to gain publicity for the cause.

1920 The League of Women Voters is founded.

1920 The Nineteenth Amendment to the Constitution, giving women the right to vote, *finally* becomes law when it is ratified by two-thirds of the states.

★ ★ ★ ★ ★ ★ ★ ★ ★ ★

Amid much gossip, they were soon married and doing everything together, and Edith was picking up politics fast. She advised him on every document that crossed his desk and shared his responsibilities. Theirs was perhaps the first true working partnership in the White House.

***

Odd Edith Facts

- Many admired her just for her handshake. It was firm, not wimpy like those of past First Ladies, who sometimes wouldn't shake hands at all, preferring only to smile and bow.
- She was a descendant of Pocahontas, and whenever she christened ships going to sea she gave them Indian names. Because Pocahontas was a Powhatan princess, Edith was treated like royalty whenever she was in Europe.
- She was the first woman in Washington who drove her own car.
- She opposed women's suffrage. She called suffragettes "disgusting" for bothering her husband. After the Nineteenth Amendment was finally passed (with Woodrow's reluctant support), she voted only once, for her husband.

***

The rest of Woodrow's time in office was dominated by World War I, as he reluctantly sent American troops to Europe to "keep the world safe for democracy." Edith set an example for the country in the necessary rationing of food and gas. She also supported Woodrow in every way, sharing each bit of war information, primarily worried about his fragile health under the dreadful strain. When the Allies met in Europe to determine the terms of peace, she traveled with him.

Upon their return, Woodrow campaigned for Senate approval of the peace treaty and the League of Nations, his dream of getting nations to come together in world peace.

Then Edith's worst fear came true. Halfway through

his second term, Woodrow suffered a severe stroke, leaving him partially paralyzed.

Staring at his helpless face, she made a momentous choice: "He must never know how ill he was, and I must carry on." Instead of allowing him to simply resign, she boldly decided she was prepared to finish out the term herself while he recuperated. To those who accused her of grabbing power, she called her role a "stewardship," never initiating programs or making major decisions. She insisted that this is what Woodrow's doctors had ordered and what he wanted.

For her actions, she has sometimes been called our first woman president. She took over routine duties and details, and for the first month she screened all visitors. She selected which matters of state to bring to her husband's limited attention, letting everything else go to the heads of the other departments.

Critics were appalled and called it a "petticoat government," another reference to women's underwear. But no one was willing to declare the president incapable of fulfilling his duties, and there was no law in place that she was breaking.

SECRET SERVICE AND FLOTUS

After McKinley's assassination in 1901, Congress directed the Secret Service to provide physical protection for presidents. During the turbulent years of World War I, Edith was the first First Lady to have full-time Secret Service protection. (Ellen, on the other hand, had liked guns and kept a revolver under her pillow at night.) The Secret Service gives nicknames to First Ladies, and all of them are referred to as FLOTUS— First Ladies of the United States.

Edith had at least one direct effect on history and it was huge: While Woodrow was incapacitated, the Senate voted down participating in the League of Nations. Some historians speculate that if she had let him resign, America would probably have been the leader in joining the peacemaking group then, which possibly could have headed off World War II.

After the Wilsons left office, Edith nursed her husband during the last three years of his life. She lived on another thirty-seven years, overseeing the publication of his papers in sixty-nine volumes and supporting a foundation that worked to establish the United Nations, the world peacekeeping organization.

★ ★ ★ ★ ★ ★ ★ ★ ★ ★ ★ ★ ★ ★ ★ ★

EDITH AND THE BILL OF RIGHTS

Over time, historians have looked less and less favorably on Edith's fateful decision to take over presidential duties. In fact, it eventually helped lead to a change in constitutional law. Out of her assumption of power came the Twenty-fifth Amendment to the Constitution, guaranteeing that when a president is incapacitated, the vice president becomes acting president, *not* the First Lady.

★ ★ ★ ★ ★ ★ ★ ★ ★ ★ ★ ★ ★ ★ ★ ★

Edith's opinion continued to matter in Washington, and she supported John F. Kennedy when he ran for president. On his icy Inauguration Day, she rode in his parade, with a flask of bourbon to keep herself warm. She died of heart failure at eighty-nine.

CHAPTER 11

Flying First Ladies

Florence Harding

Grace Coolidge

Lou Hoover

Florence Harding (served from 1921–1923)

With Warren Harding usually ranked as our worst president—he was weak, ethically challenged, and indiscreet—what do we say about his wife? Perhaps this: Her reputation might be stronger had she backed a different man.

Florence Harding (1860–1924) grew up as the daughter of the richest man in Marion, Ohio, a hardware store owner. Disappointed that she wasn't a boy, he decided to raise her as one. As soon as she could walk, she started hanging out at the store, getting used to an all-male atmosphere. Her dad became wealthier, expanding into banking and real estate, with Florence absorbing it all.

He believed that a woman should be able to provide for herself and financed Florence's thorough education. She studied things women normally didn't—math, logic, Greek, and Latin—and excelled in music. She spent so many hours practicing the piano, her fingers reportedly bled. She wanted to become a concert pianist, while her father saw her as a teacher giving piano lessons. Their fights about it could be heard out in the street, and he took to locking her out of the house when she didn't return before her curfew.

Then, when she met a young man at the roller-skating rink and ran off with him, her father had had it. He cut her off and refused to talk to her.

Divorce came soon, and Florence was left with a small son. She did indeed teach piano lessons, got an apartment of her own, and started over as an independent woman.

She married again, to the very attractive Warren Harding, who was five years younger than her. He was the publisher of the local newspaper and seemed to have potential. She entered the newspaper business as a full partner, hired its first woman reporter, and rejoiced as circulation soared.

With Florence acting as his unofficial campaign manager, Warren went on to become a national political figure. His presidential election was the first in which women could vote, and a vigorous First Lady like Florence, who did support women's suffrage, proved popular.

★   ★   ★

FLORENCE TAKES CREDIT

- "I have only one real hobby—my husband," she said about her role in advancing her husband's political career.
- "Well, Warren Harding, I have got you the presidency. What are you going to do with it?"— upon Inauguration Day.
- "I know what's best for the president; I put him in the White House," she was quoted as saying.

★   ★   ★

During their term, she threw herself into her job despite a painful kidney disease. She walked the delicate line between projecting an image of domestic bliss and wielding power. At the same time she was sharing her yummy waffle recipe with reporters and showing off her cute dog, Laddie Boy, she made her opinions known, like being firmly against the League of Nations.

She attended cabinet meetings, taking notes; amid much grumbling from Warren's aides she had a hand in his speeches. Alas, she also helped him pack the administration with pals who used their connection to the president to make a lot of money illegally, going on to be convicted of various crimes.

WOMEN BREAK THROUGH

1923 The Equal Rights Amendment, guaranteeing equal rights for women, is introduced in Congress. It's going to prove hugely controversial.

Veterans' issues were a favorite cause with her. She would plan regular events for veterans, and even stop her car and pick them up if they needed rides. Alas, the Veterans Bureau was especially riddled with corruption, with officials stealing money meant to help injured soldiers from World War I.

Florence took risks, like becoming the first First Lady to fly in a plane. With Warren she relaxed at poker parties in the White House library, where liquor, though illegal during this time of Prohibition, flowed freely. She stuck with him even when she found out he'd been having a long-term affair with her best friend (though she did once throw a piano stool at the woman).

FLORENCE SUPPORTING WOMEN

- She held press conferences just for women reporters.
- She agitated to improve conditions for working women.
- She supported the National Woman's Party, an organization that was pushing for the hot-potato Equal Rights Amendment.
- She organized a White House women's tennis championship.

She usually traveled with her husband and was with him when he died unexpectedly in California in 1923, apparently of a heart attack. News of the criminal investigations into his administration was just starting to come out.

Did Florence poison him? Probably not, but rumors flew.

She did go home and started burning his personal papers, trying unsuccessfully to stop the scandals from spreading. She died the next year at sixty-four.

Grace Coolidge (served from 1923–1929)

Grace Coolidge (1879–1957) was sincere about wanting to help others. She was working as a teacher to deaf children at the Clarke School for the Deaf when she met Calvin Coolidge.

They belonged to the same social set, boating, picnicking, playing cards. She did burst out laughing at her accidental first sight of him through his window: he was in his underwear shaving, wearing a hat to keep the hair out of his face.

Calvin was a man of notoriously few words, and "I'm going to be married to you" was his idea of a proposal. After the wedding he handed her fifty-two pairs of his socks that needed mending. They didn't have a great amount in common, and when asked later why she married him, Grace said, "Well, I thought I would get him to enjoy life and have fun, but he was not very easy to instruct in that way."

She turned out to be a tremendous asset during Calvin's rise in politics. He was a nerd, bland and shy, while she was warm and friendly. She was more popular than he.

She worked hard on his behalf and raised their two sons. She was a baseball fanatic, and she was the one who played backyard baseball with the boys, as well as taking them fishing and swimming. When Calvin Jr. died unexpectedly at sixteen, it broke her heart.

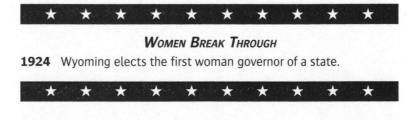

WOMEN BREAK THROUGH
1924 Wyoming elects the first woman governor of a state.

In their White House years, Calvin presided over the Roaring Twenties, a time of rapid growth. He busied himself restoring confidence in the presidency, after the scandals of his predecessor, and doing what he could to limit the size of government.

He believed women should stay in their domestic sphere. He didn't share political information with Grace and never asked her opinion, which didn't seem to bother her. He asked her not to talk about much of anything in public, especially current events, nor to do anything that would attract undue attention—no short skirts, no pants, no attractive riding clothes.

He did want her to dress stylishly. While penny-pinching about everything else, he bought her glamorous dresses in bold colors. She had to have a hat and gloves ready at all times because he would schedule formal events for her without telling her in advance.

Grace apparently didn't mind his rules: "I am rather proud of the fact . . . that my husband feels free to make his decisions and act upon them without consulting me or giving me advance information concerning them."

She continued her work with deaf children—she was delighted to welcome Helen Keller to the White House, as well as any children or veterans with disabilities.

Before he died, Calvin raised millions of dollars—and donated it all to the Clarke School for the Deaf in Grace's name as a way to honor her.

After his death she mourned, "Nobody is going to believe how I miss being told what to do."

Still, she promptly planned adventures he might have forbidden: she took her first airplane ride, wore pants, danced, bobbed her hair, rode in a car, wrote magazine articles, took her first trip to Europe. She was almost busier outside the White House than in it—serving as a trustee of the Clarke School, active in the Red Cross, and part of a committee trying to rescue Jewish children in Germany before World War II. She died at seventy-eight, still a beloved figure.

Grace Firsts and Onlies

- She was the first to receive an honorary doctorate.
- She was the first to listen to baseball games on the radio in the White House.
- She was the first to appear in a movie (for charity).
- She was the only one to be called "Sunshine" by the staff—they loved her.
- She was the only one to have a pet named Rebecca Raccoon—she kept a wide array of pets.

Lou Hoover (served from 1929–1933)

In a more prosperous era, Lou Hoover (1874–1944) might have been one of our major First Ladies. She was a force of nature herself, plus a great lover of the outdoors. Her father had taken her camping, hiking, hunting, and horseback riding. She picked Stanford University because it had the best gym. She was the only woman in the geology department there, and the first American woman to get a degree in geology.

She met Herbert in a geology lab. Besides a love of the outdoors, they both had a passion for rocks, minerals, and mining. The day after their wedding, they flew to China, where he worked as a geologist and mining engineer, scouting new sites for mines throughout rugged terrain. She was his partner, helping him with paperwork and maps, and raising their two sons, who started accompanying them as babies.

Lou was unusually accomplished—a scholar contributing original research, the recipient of several honorary degrees, and a coordinator of relief efforts for World War I refugees. She spoke five languages, including Mandarin Chinese, making her the only First Lady to speak an Asian language. But always she said that her career was helping her husband in *his* career.

She was with him every step of the way as he made a fortune of some four million dollars. When he entered politics and won a landslide presidential victory, she was our worldliest First Lady, having traveled to more countries than any other.

Eight months into their White House years, the stock market crashed. Instead of the Roaring Twenties, it was now the Great Depression, the biggest crisis to slam America since the Civil War.

The Hoovers were caught off guard and like many others underestimated the severity of the crisis. They still entertained elegantly, being extra careful about using their own money while so many people were losing theirs. With the economy spiraling downward, many blamed Herbert, which Lou found completely unfair.

LOU AND THE STAFF

The White House staff reported that the only time the Hoovers ate alone was on their wedding anniversary each year. They preferred to have company and they preferred not to see the staff. A system of three bells would ring and all the servants would have to scurry and hide. At meals Lou devised a system of hand signals so she didn't have to actually speak to the staff.

Lou became the first First Lady to give a national radio address and went on to speak regularly on the radio. Her main topic, following Herbert's lead, was volunteerism, getting people to help one another through the tough times.

She invited blacks to visit the White House and advocated for equal rights—congressmen from southern states were so offended that they threatened to have her officially censured.

WOMEN BREAK THROUGH

1932 In Arkansas, the first woman to win a Senate seat in her own right wins a special election.

A founder of the National Amateur Athletic Federation, Lou encouraged all women to be active and enjoy nature. She adored the Girl Scouts and was a devoted Scout leader for many years, eventually becoming honorary president.

She hadn't been involved in the suffrage movement. But once women were able to vote, she encouraged them to do so and joined the League of Women Voters, a group that supplied information on candidates. She urged girls to get an education and prepare for a career but believed that a couple could sustain only one career: the husband's or the wife's.

As the Depression deepened, people saw the government's actions as inadequate and grew angry. With one out of four people out of work, volunteerism wasn't enough. Herbert became the most hated man in America. After a landslide election voted him out, the disappointed Hoovers split their time between a Palo Alto home Lou had designed and an apartment in New York City.

She kept up her strenuous outdoor activities, dying of a heart attack at sixty-nine. Two hundred Girl Scouts attended her funeral.

Lou had given many speeches encouraging people to reach out to help others, but no one knew how much she was doing herself. After she died, people contacted Herbert, wondering why their checks had stopped coming. It turned out that hundreds of desperate people had been writing to the First Lady for help, and without telling anyone Lou had been sending many of them money.

CHAPTER 12

First Lady of the World

Eleanor Roosevelt

Eleanor Roosevelt (served from 1933–1945)

Among the many extraordinary things about Eleanor Roosevelt (1884–1962) was the arc of her journey: from a painfully shy girl who didn't believe women should vote or have a role in politics to a powerful activist who changed expectations of women in public. Few transformations have been as dramatic as hers.

At the age of fifteen, after a miserable childhood, neglected by her wealthy family, and frightened of everything, she encountered an inspirational teacher who changed her life: "I finally learned that I [had] a brain." The teacher gave Eleanor special attention as an intelligent, independent person and told her she expected great things from her.

At seventeen she made her debut into high society in a whirl of dances and parties. But she had a serious side too, doing volunteer work for charities in poor neighborhoods. Her growing knowledge of how the poor actually lived gave her great sensitivity to people who didn't have her many privileges.

She married distant cousin Franklin Delano Roosevelt with her uncle President Theodore Roosevelt giving her away. Most historians think the couple had never kissed before their wedding day.

For the next ten years, as his career flourished, she was having babies—six in all (one died as an infant).

Then Franklin was stricken with the dreaded disease of polio, paralyzing his legs. Eleanor nursed him devotedly. As a way to keep his interest in politics alive while others were advising him to give it up, she got active in the women's division of his political party. As he campaigned for governor and forged ahead, she became his eyes and ears, tirelessly reporting back to him. She never mentioned her secret desire—to write novels or plays—not wanting to be selfish.

★   ★   ★

EARLY ELEANOR

- **"A woman's place was not in the public eye" (in her 1937 autobiography, repeating what her grandmother taught her).**
- **"I took it for granted that men were superior creatures" (describing her shock when she found out FDR supported women's suffrage).**
- **"I suppose I was fitting pretty well into the pattern of a fairly conventional, quiet, young society matron" (from her autobiography, about the first years of her marriage).**
- **"I never wanted to be a president's wife, and I don't want it now" (to a friend just before becoming First Lady).**

★   ★   ★

He considered her "the most extraordinarily interesting woman" he had ever known. But he also cheated on her. When she found out he was having an affair with her secretary, she said, "The bottom dropped out of my own particular world. . . . I really grew up that year." A divorce would have killed his career, so they turned their marriage into more of a working partnership.

As she once explained their relationship: "He might have been happier with a wife who was completely uncritical. That I was never able to be, and he had to find it in some other people. Nevertheless, I think I sometimes acted as a spur, even though the spurring was not always wanted or welcome."

On the night of Franklin's election to president, she cried: "Now I'll have no identity." A careful observer of other First Ladies, she didn't want to be limited to a hostess role. She wanted to be useful, to do things that actually helped people.

She was quick to realize that access to the president was a gift she couldn't afford to waste. Our longest-serving First Lady, Eleanor went on to help people through twelve of the most difficult years—getting the country through the Great Depression in the 1930s and World War II in the 1940s.

At one point Eleanor craved a title of her own so she would be held accountable and know at the end of the day whether she had really made a difference. Franklin appointed her assistant director of the Office of Civilian Defense, coordinating volunteers to protect American citizens in the event of an attack during the war. But no one took her seriously—she wasn't a real employee, just someone married to the president. "Actual participation [by women] in the work of the government, we are not yet able to accept," she wrote later, explaining her resignation.

So she formed her own staff, held her own press conferences, gathered information from all parts of the country, gave lectures and radio broadcasts, and wrote a newspaper column called "My Day." Her column was full of her daily thoughts on matters great and small, especially relating to women, and was hugely popular for the comfort it brought during frightening times. During the war she traveled constantly to visit American troops and build morale.

★ ★ ★ ★ ★ ★ ★ ★ ★ ★ ★ ★ ★ ★

ELEANOR AND MONEY

After Edith Wilson, Eleanor was the second First Lady to earn her own money. She got paid for writing, lecturing (as many as a hundred lectures a year for as much as one thousand dollars each), speaking on the radio, and teaching. She drew criticism from those who disapproved, but she liked the feeling of independence it gave her. She was proud of earning her own income, which usually topped the president's, and she donated it to charities.

★ ★ ★ ★ ★ ★ ★ ★ ★ ★ ★ ★ ★ ★

She helped develop or strongly supported many of the programs in FDR's New Deal, a series of initiatives meant to restore the economy. Her particular interests were in improving housing, upholding workers' rights, supporting artists and writers, and getting federal agencies and wealthy individuals to directly help desperate people.

She was always pressuring Franklin to take action on social issues. Into an "Eleanor basket" next to his bed she put her suggestions. He learned that she could do things that he, for political reasons, couldn't. If she wanted to support the antilynching bill or have Colored Only signs taken down, he would tell her to go ahead. "I can always say I can't do a thing with you." It was a joke, but also his way of supporting her.

In one of her most famous steps, she resigned from the Daughters of the American Revolution in protest over its racism. When it barred Marian Anderson, the African American singer, from performing at its Constitution Hall, she arranged for the singer to perform at the Lincoln Memorial instead.

A major influence on her was her long friendship with Pauli Murray, a civil rights lawyer and granddaughter of a slave. At a time when discrimination was the norm, Eleanor was responsible for FDR's appointing more blacks to government positions than all the previous presidents combined—some forty-five African Americans, known as the Black Cabinet or Black Brain Trust, served as his advisers. His administration was also the most open so far to women.

★　★　★　★　★　★　★　★　★　★

WOMEN BREAK THROUGH

1933 Frances Perkins becomes FDR's secretary of labor, the first woman to serve in the U.S. cabinet.

★　★　★　★　★　★　★　★　★　★

In official photos, Eleanor was often the only woman in the picture. With the first of her many books, she called for women to get more active in politics. Her closest friendship was with Lorena Hickok, the most important political journalist of the day. Hickok sometimes lived at the White House, and over the course of thirty years, Eleanor wrote her thousands of letters.

With her depths of compassion, Eleanor advocated for civil rights for blacks, women's rights, the poor and the young, the homeless, migrant workers, Japanese Americans during World War II, Jewish refugees from Europe. She wanted to become their voice in government, a champion of the underdog.

★ ★ ★ ★ ★ ★ ★ ★ ★ ★ ★ ★ ★ ★

Best of the Best

Eleanor Roosevelt was ranked by historians in a 2014 poll as America's best First Lady—for her accomplishments in advancing women's issues, communicating, performing the greatest service to the country after leaving office, and creating a lasting legacy as an influential humanitarian.

Following Eleanor were Abigail Adams, Jacqueline Kennedy, Dolley Madison, Michelle Obama, Hillary Clinton, Lady Bird Johnson, Betty Ford, Martha Washington, and Rosalynn Carter.

The same poll also ranked Eleanor and FDR as the most effective power couple—since he was ranked the best president, they had a perfect score of 100.

★ ★ ★ ★ ★ ★ ★ ★ ★ ★ ★ ★ ★ ★

She couldn't have been less interested in house-keeping. At the White House she hired a cook who was terrible and kept her on despite all the complaints. The only dish she herself mastered was scrambled eggs, which she made once a week while her husband served cocktails to the smartest people they knew—the staff called Sunday suppers "Scrambled eggs with brains."

After FDR's death in office, she returned to a cottage at their estate, saying, "The story is over." But within a year she was back on the world stage as an activist in her own right.

★   ★   ★

AN ADMIRER

"I am a die-hard Eleanor Roosevelt fan."
—Hillary Clinton

★   ★   ★

The next president, Harry Truman, appointed her one of the first five American delegates to the United Nations, which she saw as the world's best hope for a lasting peace. Her greatest accomplishment there was the Universal Declaration of Human Rights, an agreement meant to protect the dignity and equal rights of all people. In her spare time she kept up with her twenty-three grandchildren and great-grandchildren and helped select books for the Junior Literary Guild.

AMERICAN ENEMY NUMBER 1?

Did everyone like Eleanor? Definitely not. The fiercest of her enemies was probably FBI director J. Edgar Hoover. He found her stand on civil rights for African Americans such a threat to American society and values that he had her followed everywhere. The FBI file on Eleanor Roosevelt is one of its largest—three thousand pages.

She was the most criticized First Lady in history. Enemies accused her of stimulating racial prejudices, meddling in politics, talking too much, being too informal. Cruel jokes ridiculed her appearance and high-pitched voice. Many people wrote furious letters to FDR, urging that she be muzzled and kept on a chain.

She even received numerous death threats. The Secret Service, worried about her safety, taught her how to shoot. But she kept the gun (unloaded) in the glove compartment of her car and refused to tolerate more than just one bodyguard.

Eleanor declined various offers to run for office, notably that of president. She thought the country wouldn't be ready for a woman president for a long time.

But she was influential in supporting candidates she approved of.

By the end of her life, people were calling her "the first lady of the world." She was an inspiration for young women, who saw her doing things women had never done before. She died at seventy-eight after her heart failed.

Eleanor Roosevelt was going to be one very tough act to follow.

★   ★   ★

LATER ELEANOR

- "As a rule women know not only what men know, but much that men will never know" (from a "My Day" column in 1937).
- "No one can make you feel inferior without your consent" (from her autobiography).
- "Every woman in public life needs to develop skin as tough as rhinoceros hide" (in 1936, responding to critics who mocked her visibility).
- "The battle for the individual rights of women is one of long-standing and none of us should countenance anything which undermines it" (from a 1941 "My Day" column).
- "Having learned to stare down fear, I long ago reached the point where there is no living person whom I fear, and few challenges that I am not willing to face" (from her autobiography).

★   ★   ★

CHAPTER 13

Pink and Pretty

Bess Truman

Mamie Eisenhower

Bess Truman (served from 1945–1953)

The next few First Ladies didn't really try to fill Eleanor's shoes. Plus the postwar era of the 1950s was a repressive time for women, locking them into stereotyped roles of being pretty, not making waves, and pleasing their husbands.

Bess Truman (1885–1982) liked sports. She was the best tennis player in town and also excelled at baseball, ice-skating, and horseback riding. She did the usual ladylike things too, like taking dancing lessons and learning social graces, and did well at school. At age eighteen, when her father committed suicide, she began parenting her younger brothers, taking care of her mother, and cultivating a sense of privacy that never went away.

She first met Harry Truman in Sunday school, when she was five and he was six. He played no sports, but they both loved to read. They waited exactly thirty years to marry while he tried to establish himself in a career.

Politics turned out to be the area where Harry's career took off. This wouldn't have been Bess's first choice, but she was the ultimate supportive wife.

THE BOSS

Bess was another First Lady to earn her own money—but it was as Harry's secretary while he was a senator. In response to lots of criticism about paying a family member, he insisted that she earned "every cent I pay her." She ran his office so superbly that he started referring to her as "the Boss."

Reluctant to be a public figure herself, doting on her daughter, Margaret, she shared her thoughts and interests in private. Harry often ended his campaign speeches by introducing her as "the Boss" (and Margaret as "the Boss's Boss").

She conscientiously fulfilled her duties as First Lady, but only the necessary ones. Besides playing bridge, she held classes for herself and other Washington wives to learn Spanish. She finally fired Eleanor's bad cook, who was still serving awful food, for not letting her take a stick of butter to her bridge club lunch.

Bess and Other First Ladies

When asked which First Lady she most identified with, Bess would say Elizabeth Monroe—the one who had the misfortune to follow dynamo Dolley Madison. Eleanor Roosevelt's footprints were large indeed. Before she left office, she had thoughtfully set up Bess's first press conference. Such a thing was not up Bess's alley at all, and she canceled it.

Bess pushed no particular cause of her own, but she was always there for Harry. Indeed, she said, "A woman's place in public is to sit beside her husband, be silent, and be sure that her hat is on straight." She burned her letters, which might have revealed more about her role. She gave only one recorded interview in her life.

She welcomed Harry home each night with cocktails, prepared to chat about his day. He was trying to fill FDR's shoes, dealing with the final weeks of World War II, the postwar economy, the Korean War, racial integration of the military, and the Red Scare—the fear of threats from the Communist Soviet Union. The whole time, he relied on Bess for constant advice (though it's not clear if she knew in advance about his decision to drop the atomic bomb to end the war).

She was religious about attending Margaret's appearances as a concert singer—she and Harry did so much with Margaret that the staff called them the three musketeers. The one career goal Bess never wanted Margaret to have was to be president.

One day, the leg of one of Margaret's pianos went through the floor of her room. The White House had started falling apart. Other floors collapsed, and chandeliers swung wildly over a reception if anyone was taking a bath upstairs. The Trumans moved across the street, and the White House was rebuilt piece by piece with enough concrete and steel to make it last. Bess wasn't overly involved with the decisions, believing that it was the nation's house, not hers.

On their last day in office, her smile was huge as she turned over the keys to her good friend Mamie Eisenhower and showed her around.

She couldn't wait to get back to their Victorian mansion in their hometown of Independence, Missouri. She loved her privacy so much that she refused to allow Secret Service agents on the property. She worked on Harry's memoirs with him, and both hung out at the local public library. She read many more books (especially the murder mysteries written by Margaret) until her death.

That day, the *New York Times* headline read "Bess Truman is dead at 97; was president's 'full partner.'"

BESS'S LONG LIFE

Bess continues to hold the record for longest-lived First Lady (or president). While many First Ladies were sickly, it turns out a large number of them have lived well into their eighties and nineties—longer than the average population. The list includes Edith Wilson, Anna Harrison, Sarah Polk, Edith Roosevelt, Lucretia Garfield, Mamie Eisenhower, Lady Bird Johnson, Pat Nixon, Betty Ford, and Nancy Reagan. Rosalynn Carter and Barbara Bush could break Bess's record.

Mamie Eisenhower (served from 1953–1961)

Like Bess Truman, Mamie Eisenhower (1896–1979) had no real cause of her own. And that was fine with Dwight Eisenhower, who'd made it clear from the start that his country came before her. "I have only one career," Mamie said, "and his name is Ike."

They had met at Fort Sam Houston, where he was a young second lieutenant on his first tour of duty. He found her "saucy in the look about her face and in her whole attitude." She proved to be an ideal army wife, following him to posts in the United States, the Panama Canal Zone (her least favorite time), France, and the Philippines.

Mamie once estimated that in thirty-seven years she had packed and unpacked their household at least twenty-seven times—once three times in one year. She never learned to cook—that was Ike's department. All the while she raised their sons, Icky and John. When Icky died at three of scarlet fever, it crushed his parents.

Each move meant increasing responsibilities for her, as Dwight took another step in his career, all the way to the top: supreme commander of the Allied Forces in Europe in 1943. His mission: to bring the nightmarish World War II to a close. To relieve the tension, she threw excellent parties with lots of card playing and people singing around the piano while she played. She wasn't always steady on her feet, and some thought she had a drinking problem, but she was actually suffering from an inner-ear disorder.

Once Ike led the Allies to victory, emerging as the most popular man in America, Mamie threw herself into his campaign for president. She was bubbly and so popular that he never appeared without her. "I like Ike" said some campaign buttons, while others said "But I LOVE MAMIE." It was the first election in which the number of women voters caught up with the number of men.

Once in the White House, she took a backseat while he made decisions during the postwar period of general peace and prosperity. She was known to visit him in the Oval Office just four times. She stuck to her homemaker role and continued to host marvelous parties, on a budget, clipping coupons for the staff.

She never spoke of politics but indicated her support of civil rights: making a point of having Marian Anderson sing at the inauguration, asking gospel singer Mahalia Jackson to sing at her birthday party, and ensuring that the annual White House Easter Egg Roll was fully integrated. She showed her disapproval of Senator Joseph McCarthy, who was persecuting people he thought were Communists, by never inviting him to the White House. She raised money for the American Heart Association, which was ironic because she smoked cigarettes, a leading cause of heart disease.

WOMEN BREAK THROUGH

1955 The arrest of Rosa Parks, an activist with the National Association for the Advancement of Colored People (NAACP), becomes a turning point in the civil rights movement.

Mamie liked her sleep: "Every woman over fifty should stay in bed until noon" was her beauty tip. She and Ike were both fascinated by the latest invention, TV, and often had dinner on trays while watching their respective shows on his and her TVs. The comedy *I Love Lucy* was a favorite, and the staff learned never to schedule anything for her during the soap opera *As the World Turns*.

If Ike got irritated when she showed up late for dinner, she would explain, "I've been busy making myself pretty for my husband." She loved clothes and jewelry, and above all she loved pink—pink bows and ribbons, pink decor. Every single thing in her bedroom including the wastebasket was pink. A pale shade called Mamie pink became all the rage in products around the country.

★ ★ ★ ★ ★ ★ ★ ★ ★ ★ ★ ★ ★

CAMP DAVID

Mamie was the first First Lady to urge her husband to make regular use of the presidential weekend retreat. Out in the country in Maryland, its lodges and cabins are meant to be an oasis of tranquility, an escape from stress. The Eisenhowers renamed it after their grandson David, and all presidents since then have relaxed or hosted important meetings there. A top-secret location, it's not on local maps.

★ ★ ★ ★ ★ ★ ★ ★ ★ ★ ★ ★ ★

She never once doubted Ike's faithfulness, even after rumors surfaced that he'd had an affair with his driver in Europe.

While still in the White House they bought a farm in Gettysburg, Pennsylvania, and began fixing up their dream retirement home. It was the first home they had ever owned.

Mamie outlived Ike by ten years, dying at eighty-two after a stroke. When asked how she wanted to be remembered, she said, "Just as a good friend."

CHAPTER 14

One Thousand Days—and Beyond

Jacqueline Kennedy

Jacqueline Kennedy (served from 1961–1963)

After the two staid First Ladies before her, Jacqueline Kennedy (1929–1994) was like magic—a gust of fresh air, youth, elegance, and optimism.

As a child Jackie learned to ride horses almost as soon as she could walk. She took ballet lessons, wrote poems and stories, and studied at the best private schools. One headmistress said, "She has the most inquiring mind we've had in thirty-five years." In college she spent her junior year in France, adored all things French, and graduated with a degree in French literature. She read up to ten books a week, trying to balance her "real hunger for knowledge" with advice from those who told her to hide her intelligence from men.

JACKIE'S JOB NUMBER 1

After college she took more classes in American history, as well as a job as the Inquiring Camera Girl for a Washington newspaper. She was to approach strangers on the street, ask a thought-provoking question, and take their pictures. One day her path crossed that of Senator John F. Kennedy, the most eligible bachelor in town. Soon she was quitting her job and bringing him hot lunches in a picnic basket.

After a glamorous wedding to JFK, she had two adorable children, Caroline and John Jr., while John soared ahead in politics. Compared to arts and literature, Jackie found politics a little tedious—she didn't even vote until she cast a vote for her husband. But she defined her role as "to take care of the president" and her children. "If you bungle raising your children, I don't think whatever else you do well matters very much." She spent as much time with her kids as possible and allowed them any pets they wanted—nine dogs at one point.

Both so charismatic and young, the Kennedys brought a spirit to the White House that made many feel excited and hopeful about the country changing for the better. The Kennedy administration deepened America's involvement in the Vietnam War, but also made strides in promoting civil rights for African Americans, inspiring young people to get involved (JFK founded the Peace Corps), slowing the nightmarish nuclear arms race, and encouraging the exploration of space.

Jackie's first move was to get rid of Mamie pink—she hated it. In her first month she created the White House Arts Committee, raising money to turn the building into a museum of American history. She gave the first-ever televised tour of the mansion in 1962, subtly making the point that this was a house of great sophistication and that America was a great superpower.

She spoke in a soft breathy voice favored by movie stars like Marilyn Monroe as a way of appearing nonthreatening to men. But her show was a big deal—90 percent of Americans now had black-and-white TVs, and people all over the world watched the first woman ever to host a TV documentary.

In fashion, millions of women copied her every move— above-the-elbow gloves, pillbox hats, a triple strand of white pearls, her trademark oversize sunglasses. She got lots of mail about her hair, which made her twitch: "What does my hairdo have to do with my husband's ability to be president?"

More important, she inspired a greater national attention to culture. She brought the most famous people in the arts and sciences to the White House for special events and served on committees supporting ballet companies and symphony orchestras.

She liked to say that "people have told me ninety-nine things that I had to do as First Lady, and I haven't done one of them!" Jackie herself was clueless about cooking, but supervised the kitchen to produce memorable meals of such delicacies as lobster cardinale and strawberries romanoff.

WOMEN BREAK THROUGH

1961 Eleanor Roosevelt notes that out of JFK's first 240 appointments, just nine are women. He establishes the President's Commission on the Status of Women and appoints her chair. It's considered the birth of what becomes known as the women's movement, or women's liberation.

1963 The Equal Pay Act makes it illegal for companies to pay different amounts to women and men who do the same work.

Jackie cultivated an air of mystery, doling out images of her family with care: "My press relations will be minimum information," she said, "given with maximum politeness." To avoid the press, she would put on a wig to take her children to movies and amusement parks.

She helped JFK with her shrewd observations of people, and on foreign trips she dazzled people with her ability to speak several languages and with her extensive knowledge of each place she visited. She was so loved in France that JFK introduced himself as "the man who accompanied Jacqueline Kennedy to Paris." During the Cuban missile crisis in 1962, when America faced a possible nuclear attack from the Soviet Union, she kept up his spirits and refused his request to leave him and take shelter in an underground bunker.

But she mostly left the politics to him. She didn't even attend public functions unless she absolutely had to, taking her children to stay for long periods at her farm in Virginia's horse country. Lady Bird Johnson, the vice president's wife, would step in to take her place as hostess, even at the last minute, when Jackie would be tempted away by a new ballet performance or other event.

She and JFK had separate bedrooms; hers was in shades of pale blue and green and filled with French and fashion magazines. He probably had more affairs than any other president, and she waved away the rumors: "I don't think there are any men who are faithful to their wives."

In 1963, after their two-day-old son Patrick died, she sought solace on a cruise with her sister around the Mediterranean on a yacht owned by a wealthy Greek businessman. When she came back she told JFK she wanted more of a role in his political life. He asked her to join him for his upcoming trip to Texas, much to the delight of the state's governor: "You'll have to bring Mrs. Kennedy because she is so popular; you'll have much bigger crowds."

Alas, the trip was to Dallas. JFK was shot and killed while sitting next to Jackie in an open car. She was traumatized, and so was the whole nation. During the aftermath and the funeral, watched around the country on the ever-present TV, she was a symbol of strength, helping the country to cope with the death of the young president.

She was still only thirty-four, with no job, no mate, and no home. After staying at the White House for two weeks, she moved on, eventually to an apartment in New York City.

★ ★ ★ ★ ★ ★ ★ ★ ★ ★ ★ ★ ★ ★

CAMELOT

After JFK's death, Jackie shaped the one thousand days of his administration into the lustrous image of the mythical King Arthur's court at Camelot. The popular musical *Camelot* was running on Broadway during this time, extolling a land where the idealistic knights of the Round Table did bold, brave deeds for "one brief shining moment."

★ ★ ★ ★ ★ ★ ★ ★ ★ ★ ★ ★ ★ ★

Five years later, after JFK's brother Robert was also assassinated, Jackie grew disgusted with the country and fearful for her and her children's safety. She married that Greek businessman, Aristotle Onassis. He was much older and not as glamorous as her, but he had his own island, Skorpios. She tried to work on a TV project, but he said, "No Greek wife works." Nicknamed "Jackie O," she spent the school year with her children in New York, jetted around Europe, and kept up with her reading. "All she does is read," Onassis once complained.

After he died, she told a friend, "I have always lived through men. Now I realize I can't do that anymore." She returned to her apartment in New York in 1978 and started a whole new career.

In college she had dreamed of writing the great American novel. Now she helped other writers with their books—as an editor for publishing companies.

JACKIE'S JOB NUMBER 2

After her first week in her new job she came up with a list of twenty possible book projects. Her very first book was a nod to First Lady Abigail Adams: *"Remember the Ladies": Women in America, 1750–1815*. She went on to publish dozens of books about art, history, literature, and pop culture. Her books with celebrities included Michael Jackson's *Moonwalk*. The first First Lady to have a distinguished career post White House, she dedicated herself to making the world a better place through literature, her true love.

She described her new life as "very ordinary," far different from being First Lady. She jogged through Central Park every day, took yoga classes, did her own shopping at the local grocery store, went to events with a longtime boyfriend, and at work made her own coffee, did her own Xeroxing, answered her own phone. She refused to write her memoirs, saying that she wanted to live her life, not record it.

For her new career and the dignity she had shown after the assassination, Jackie became a hero to the women's movement. She remains possibly our most fascinating First Lady: by the time she died of cancer at sixty-four, there were already twenty-two biographies of her in print.

In a class of her own, Jacqueline Kennedy continues to beguile us.

CHAPTER 15

A Millionaire, a Goodwill Ambassador, and One Who Made a Difference

Lady Bird Johnson

Pat Nixon

Betty Ford

Lady Bird Johnson (served from 1963–1969)

The next three First Ladies made their way through the noise and confusion of the 1960s and 1970s, with its upheaval in many parts of the culture (including views of women), more assassinations and attempts, and demonstrations against the increasingly unpopular Vietnam War.

When shy Lady Bird Johnson (1912–2007) realized she was about to graduate first in her high school class, she deliberately let her grades slip. She didn't want to have to give the traditional valedictorian speech. Later, she was a star student at the University of Texas. Earning degrees with honors in arts and journalism, she graduated at the top of her class. She was planning a career in the media— presumably not as a speaker.

Then she met a hopeful young politician, Lyndon Johnson. They both loved to dance. On their second date he proposed, and eventually at age twenty-one she accepted. "Sometimes Lyndon simply takes your breath away."

As independent as she was, she got used to being dominated by her husband. She had to shine his shoes, bring him breakfast in bed, make sure his cigarette lighter was filled, learn to cook, and help with the details of his work. While he was in the navy, she ran his congressional office (without pay).

LADY BIRD'S MONEY

Lady Bird financed Lyndon's campaigns. After she inherited some money, she bought an unsuccessful radio station and turned it around, expanding it into a media empire. It made her a millionaire, the first First Lady to make a million on her own. At a time when few women worked outside the home, she was a shrewd investor and manager—a pioneer.

She took years of public speaking lessons and got more comfortable in the limelight. As the wife of the vice president, she was an ambassador of goodwill, visiting thirty-three foreign countries. People admired the gracious way she stood in for Jackie at official events.

After JFK's assassination, she was a reluctant First Lady, but she put a motivating sign on her desk—Can Do.

When Lyndon ran in the next election, she campaigned with flair—on a train called the Lady Bird Special. She became the first First Lady to take a train trip to campaign on her own. She traveled for four days through racially divided areas where it was considered too dangerous for Lyndon to appear.

This was a big deal—Lyndon's staff disapproved, unaware of her strength. In eight states, she gave forty-seven formal speeches. Her message was that the Civil War was over and the South had to move on into the modern world. Amid constant bomb and death threats, with the Secret Service all over her, she never showed fear, meeting hecklers with poise, dignity, and sometimes anger. Many credited LBJ's victory to her.

She took an active part in his War on Poverty program, his plan to reduce the high poverty rate still plaguing America. Her special interest was the Head Start project for preschool children, and she traveled the country promoting it. To LBJ she urged the advancement of women: "Well, what did you do for women today?" she would ask him each night.

Her main interest became beautification—environmental protection and preservation as a way of convincing people to actively participate in their communities. She personally lobbied Congress for money to finance her ideas. She created the Committee for a More Beautiful Capital, then expanded it into a national program. Her work led to the Highway Beautification Act of 1965, which limited outdoor advertising and provided funding for cleanup.

Women Break Through

1964 Patsy Mink of Hawaii is the first Asian American woman elected to Congress.

1964 Margaret Chase Smith becomes the first woman to run for a U.S. presidential nomination on a major party ticket.

1964 Title VII of the Civil Rights Act prohibits discrimination in employment on the basis of race or sex.

1966 National Organization for Women is founded to enforce full equality for women in truly equal partnership with men.

1968 Shirley Chisholm is the first black woman elected to Congress.

1969 Yale and Princeton finally accept female students, followed by Harvard in 1977.

She allowed her daughters, Lynda Bird and Luci, to host dance parties demonstrating the frug, the monkey, the Watusi, and all the latest moves. She didn't cook, and when traveling with her black cook, she refused to stay at any hotels that wouldn't house them both.

People started to compare her to Eleanor Roosevelt, thrilling her to no end because Eleanor was her role model.

At the same time, she always deferred to her overbearing husband. She told the staff, "My husband comes first, the girls second, and I will be satisfied with what's left." When asked about his affairs with other women, she said, "The public should weigh what public servants are doing, not their private, innermost feelings." She believed that citizens didn't need to know every little thing about those in government.

They remained affectionate, and he often grabbed her for a kiss. They shared in the care of their two beagles, Him and Her. "He made me more than I would have been," she said. "I offered him some peace and quiet, maybe a little judgment."

He once admitted that voters "would happily have elected her over me." His escalation of the war in Vietnam diminished his popularity, not so much hers. She played little role in his foreign policy, supported it in public, and was calm when she had to face demonstrators herself.

Later, after he died, she still gave speeches—"I don't want to shut myself up"—founded the National Wildflower Research Center, and served on the board of trustees of the National Geographic Society.

Lady Bird had found her voice and became a beloved figure. After her death at ninety-four, members of eight presidential families attended her funeral.

Pat Nixon (served from 1969–1974)

"I've never had it easy," Pat Nixon (1912–1993) once said.

Growing up on a small farm, she worked from an unusually early age, at twelve taking care of her brothers when her mom died. She nursed her father until he died when she was eighteen. On her own, she worked her way through the University of Southern California. Always resourceful, she took various jobs—as a department store sales clerk and as an extra in the movies—graduating with honors.

She was teaching high school when she met a young lawyer, Richard Nixon. At the local community theater, they were cast in the same play, *The Dark Tower*. He told her right away that he was going to marry her. She thought he was "nuts," but he wore her down after two years—even back then she was saying she thought he'd be president someday.

During World War II, she worked as a government economist while he served in the navy. Afterward, she agreed to let him enter politics on the strict condition that she never have to give a speech and that their family life would be kept private. Six hours after her first baby was born, she was typing and researching his speeches.

When he told her he was running for governor she ran crying from the table. She hated being a political wife, but it turned out she was very good at it. She ended up campaigning at his side as well as behind the scenes, all while raising two daughters.

Once in the White House, Pat was determined to make the best of it, even though "being the First Lady is the hardest unpaid job in the world." When asked what her focus was she said, "People." She used her position to encourage volunteer service—"the spirit of people helping people."

Pat's Coat

Being part of his team meant having to stand by Richard's side during crises. When he was accused of taking illegal contributions during an election, she dutifully stood beside him as he defended himself on TV.

Pat didn't dress in fancy minks, he pointed out, but in a respectable cloth coat. This was his famous Checkers speech, in which he did refuse to return the family dog, Checkers, who'd been given to them by a supporter.

She also did much on a personal level, particularly at Thanksgiving. She hosted a special holiday meal for senior citizens who had no families to go to, and another for wounded and disabled veterans. She saw handing out her Thanksgiving recipes as a way of humanizing her husband, who often seemed chilly. (When asked about this, she would say, "Oh, but you just don't realize how much fun he is . . . he's just so much fun!")

Sometimes people mocked her as "plastic Pat." But that's how she was, usually calm. "I detest scenes. I just can't be that way," she told a daughter. Staff would sometimes spot the First Couple holding hands when they thought no one was looking. But mostly they were known for not being physically affectionate. Once on her birthday she reached out to hug him and he turned away.

★ ★ ★ ★ ★ ★ ★ ★ ★ ★ ★ ★ ★ ★ ★ ★

Pat and Pandas

She shared her husband's often harrowing foreign visits in his vice presidential and presidential years. These included crucial meetings in the Soviet Union, as well as the visit to the People's Republic of China, a historic step forward in relations with China. A lifelong smoker of cigarettes (in private, not public), she pointed one day to a cigarette pack with a picture of pandas on it. Because of her gesture, misunderstood as a request for actual pandas, America got its first two pandas.

★ ★ ★ ★ ★ ★ ★ ★ ★ ★ ★ ★ ★ ★ ★ ★

When Richard spoke about issues, she scheduled trips afterward that would highlight those issues. If he gave a speech about crime, she toured facilities for juvenile criminals. When he addressed the energy crisis, she visited model homes built to conserve energy.

She also took journeys on her own as an ambassador of goodwill—our most-traveled First Lady at the time. Her first solo trip was to take relief supplies to earthquake victims in Peru. She was the first First Lady to visit a combat zone (South Vietnam) and Africa (Ghana, Liberia, and the Ivory Coast).

As for women's causes, she wanted Richard to appoint a woman to the Supreme Court—and stopped speaking to him for a while when he chose yet another man. She supported the Equal Rights Amendment, and wore pants in defiance of his dislike of women wearing pants. She took yoga lessons in the White House as part of a women's health education program.

"I just want to be remembered as the wife of the president," Pat said, but in fact she was much more popular than he was. He had a dim view of women—the president needs "a wife who's intelligent, but not too intelligent," he said—but did come around to believing that a woman would be president within fifty years.

WOMEN BREAK THROUGH

1971 *Ms. Magazine* first appears; three hundred thousand copies are sold out in eight days. "Ms." was a new term for women who didn't want to identify themselves by their relationship to a man by using either "Miss" or "Mrs." The magazine, owned and operated by women, was a way for feminist ideas to reach a much wider audience.

1971 The Boston Women's Health Book Collective publishes their groundbreaking book about women's health, *Our Bodies, Ourselves*.

1972 Title IX of the Education Amendments bans sex discrimination in any federally funded school activities. Enrollment of women in athletics programs increases dramatically.

1973 The Supreme Court, with *Roe v. Wade*, protects a woman's right to an abortion (reversing Congress's 1830 decision to outlaw abortion, which had up until then been legal, if unsafe).

1973 Women are finally allowed to serve on juries in all fifty states.

1974 The Equal Credit Opportunity Act makes it illegal to refuse a credit card to a woman based on her gender.

Richard was one president who went overboard in recording his activities for posterity, installing an elaborate taping system around the White House. Pat had advised him to burn his tapes, but he didn't listen. During the Watergate scandal—named for the hotel where allies trying to get him reelected broke in and illegally wiretapped the phones—his tapes became public. He was forced to resign for attempting to cover up criminal acts, the only president to resign in disgrace.

He called his staff asking for packing boxes—that's how they discovered the news—and the couple left the White House together, as a team.

Pat went into seclusion. She died at eighty-one of lung cancer. Richard cried uncontrollably during the funeral and died ten months later.

Betty Ford (served from 1974–1977)

Betty Ford (1918–2011) was her own person—a particular challenge when serving as First Lady. But that's not something she ever predicted she'd be.

She started out as a dancer. After studying modern dance at college, she wanted to make it a career, and was accepted into Martha Graham's famous concert troupe in New York City. While performing at places like Carnegie Hall, she supported herself as a fashion model.

Moving back to her hometown of Grand Rapids, Michigan, she was a fashion coordinator for a department store and kept up with her dancing—organizing her own dance group and teaching dance to disabled children. Her first marriage was unhappy and ended in divorce after five years.

She began dating Gerald Ford, a lawyer on his way into the House of Representatives. With not all voters approving of a divorced ex-dancer, he asked her to postpone the wedding until he was sure he'd win. In a happy, affectionate marriage, raising their four children, she was caught off guard when Richard Nixon selected Jerry as his running mate, and then even more startled when Jerry became president upon Nixon's humiliating resignation.

At the White House, Betty greeted the staff enthusiastically (something they weren't used to); danced her way through parties; and was once able to dance with her idol, Fred Astaire. She also campaigned hard for Jerry when needed and helped as he recovered from the scare of two assassination attempts. Within one three-week period, in unrelated incidents, two women tried to shoot him and failed.

Her sense of humor was a treat: "You've heard me

say many times whatever makes Jerry happy makes me happy," she told reporters, adding slyly, "if you *believe* that, you're indeed unworthy of your profession."

★ ★ ★ ★ ★ ★ ★ ★ ★ ★ ★ ★ ★ ★

BETTY'S PILLOW TALK

She was the first First Lady to admit to using pillow talk—nighttime chats while sharing the same bed with her husband—to get her points across. She wanted a woman in the cabinet and on the Supreme Court. While watching her interviewed on TV—talking about how she supported the Equal Rights Amendment (ERA) and a woman's right to choose—he knew she was costing him votes and playfully threw a pillow *at* her. "I don't believe being First Lady should prevent me from expressing my ideas," she always insisted.

★ ★ ★ ★ ★ ★ ★ ★ ★ ★ ★ ★ ★ ★

After six weeks as First Lady, she was diagnosed with breast cancer. At the time, this was a subject that made many uncomfortable and just wasn't talked about in public. But Betty spoke frankly about her diagnosis, her mastectomy, and the importance of early detection. Her bold example inspired untold numbers of other women to learn about the disease and get more checkups.

Just as she was unusually honest about being divorced (still considered taboo by some) and her cancer, she didn't mind saying she was under stress. She described the role of First Lady as "much more of a twenty-four-hour job than anyone would guess." In fact, she told the press, "I take a Valium every day," admitting to using tranquilizers.

Eventually, after her family held two interventions, she acknowledged a problem with drugs and alcohol and went into treatment. After her recovery, always wanting to help others, she went public in a big way and established the Betty Ford Center for treatment of chemical dependency. The effect was to reduce the stigma of addiction, shedding light into dark corners of people's lives, showing that help was available. Today, having helped over one hundred thousand people, hers is considered one of the best treatment centers in the world.

WOMEN BREAK THROUGH

1975 Women are permitted to enroll in the U.S. military academies for the first time.

1975 The first marital rape law passes in South Dakota, making it illegal for a husband to rape his wife—not criminalized in all states until 1993.

1977 A court rules in favor of a woman fired for refusing her boss's sexual advances—the first time sexual harassment is recognized as legitimate grounds for a legal complaint. Three years later, the Equal Employment Opportunity Commission formally defines sexual harassment.

Comfortable on a stage, she continued her work as an advocate for breast cancer awareness and as active chair of the board of directors for the Betty Ford Center, as well as passionate supporter of the ERA.

She died at ninety-three, another reluctant First Lady, but one who made a genuine difference.

CHAPTER 16

The Steel Magnolia, the Iron Butterfly, and the Enforcer

Rosalynn Carter

Nancy Reagan

Barbara Bush

Rosalynn Carter (served from 1977–1981)

Rosalynn Carter (1927–) seems shy and retiring at first glance, but she's not to be underestimated. She is one of only four First Ladies who's made it into the National Women's Hall of Fame (the others being Abigail Adams, Eleanor Roosevelt, and Hillary Clinton).

When she was thirteen, she lost her father. She helped with her mother's dressmaking business, as well as the housekeeping and care of her three younger siblings. Times were hard, but she got herself to Georgia Southwestern State University. She dreamed of being an architect or interior designer.

She left school after being swept off her feet by Jimmy Carter, an old family friend and neighbor, and a navy officer. Their first fight was years into their marriage, when he resigned from the navy to take over his family's peanut farm. Rosalynn strongly opposed the move but lost. Soon she was doing the farm's accounts, and then working full-time managing the business and raising their four children while he began running for office.

Speaking in public made her sick. But she worked hard to overcome the fear and took part in all his campaigning, becoming known fondly as the "steel magnolia." Jimmy called her "almost a perfect extension of myself."

On the way to the White House on Inauguration Day, they walked hand in hand down Pennsylvania Avenue. They were showing their partnership as well as their commitment to conserving energy by not riding in a car.

★　　★　　★

A RARE STATEMENT

"I enjoyed every minute of it," Rosalynn said of her years as First Lady.

★　　★　　★

She attended cabinet meetings and major briefings. "Ros, what think?" Jimmy would write on all his policy papers. She advised him as he dealt with one crisis after another: a recession—a time of high unemployment and little economic growth—as well as an energy crisis, when the cost of oil soared, and worsening relations with Iran, which took fifty-two Americans hostage for over a year.

She also frequently represented him at ceremonies and served as his personal ambassador to Latin American countries. Many were shocked at her active role, but they noticed that she strengthened ties wherever she visited. She impressed dignitaries with her ability to speak Spanish and her extensive knowledge of world affairs.

She advocated for numerous causes, especially mental health. She gave many press conferences on her own, showing irritation only when the questions were trivial—about fashion, for example. She kept her cool at embarrassing moments. After he said in an interview that he had never cheated on her but had only lusted after other women in his heart, she said, "Jimmy talks too much."

Women Break Through

1978 With the Pregnancy Discrimination Act, women can no longer be fired from their workplace for being pregnant.

They lived more simply than most First Couples. While setting an example to conserve energy, he kept the White House so cold that the staff took pity on

Rosalynn and bought her some long underwear. She wore polyester off-the-rack dresses, and the couple asked to be served leftovers for their personal meals. Fiercely opposed to segregation, she hired as her daughter Amy's nanny a black woman who she believed had been unfairly convicted of murder, later making sure she got a full pardon. Amy went to public school, not the private schools First Couples usually choose.

★ ★ ★ ★ ★ ★ ★ ★ ★ ★ ★ ★ ★

Rosalynn and Women

She used her influence to urge Jimmy to appoint more women to senior government positions. Almost one in four political appointments during their administration went to women—a record. She worked hard for the passage of the ERA and was crushed when it failed to be ratified. She refused to be a member of any church that didn't allow women to be pastors.

★ ★ ★ ★ ★ ★ ★ ★ ★ ★ ★ ★ ★

As the crises dragged on, Jimmy grew increasingly unpopular. After he lost his reelection bid and seemed to take it in stride, she said, "I'm bitter enough for both of us." She was vocal about her disapproval of his successor—unusual in a First Lady.

But once they left, she morphed into one of our most activist former First Ladies. She leads programs to promote greater access to mental health care. She cofounded the Carter Center in Atlanta, which does important work in resolving conflict and improving global health. Among other accomplishments, the center led a campaign to all but eradicate the dreaded Guinea worm disease from Africa and Asia. In 2015, thanks to her prodding, Jimmy dedicated the rest of his life to fighting for women's rights worldwide.

She wrote one book with Jimmy and said never again—their styles were so different that they stopped speaking and took to leaving nasty messages for each other. Today she writes her own books.

She is also active in Habitat for Humanity, an organization for building affordable housing, working as an architect and interior designer in her own way.

Nancy Reagan (served from 1981–1989)

Nancy Reagan (1921–2016) was a theater person—not just a theater lover like Mary Lincoln and others but an actor on stage. Her mother was an actor who had legendary movie stars hanging around the house. In high school Nancy performed in many plays, including one called *First Lady*, and in college she majored in theater.

In her first appearance on film, she played a volunteer in the fight against polio. It was a short film shown in theaters to raise money for a group headed by Eleanor Roosevelt. She went on to appear in eleven feature films, and then within a year of arriving in Hollywood, she met the president of the Screen Actors Guild, fellow actor Ronald Reagan.

She gladly gave up an acting career for the starring role as his wife and the mother to their children. "My life really began when I married my husband," she said. She supported his move up the political ladder, making her views about appointments and policy very clear, earning enemies among men who called her Iron Butterfly and other nicknames.

★   ★   ★

NANCY AND WOMEN

- **"A woman's real happiness and real fulfillment come from within the home with her husband and children" (after retiring from acting in 1952).**
- **"However the First Lady fits in, she has a unique and important role to play in looking after her husband. And it's only natural that she'll let him know what she thinks. I always do that for Ronnie and I always will" (in her 1989 memoirs).**

★   ★   ★

Once in the theater of the national stage, she hosted parties full of Hollywood stars and spent many hours visiting veterans, the elderly, and the emotionally and physically handicapped. But her main issue was Ronald's health. She always insisted that he get his rest and keep to a regular routine, even pulling him out of meetings if necessary. She was heard yelling at him if he stayed up too late watching TV.

Then, sixty-nine days into their administration, Ronald was shot and seriously wounded in an assassination attempt. Though he quickly recovered, the trauma resulted in a great weight loss for her and increased anxiety about his well-being. One thing she turned to was astrology, using it to determine which days seemed dangerous for him to appear in public and which seemed safe. Other First Ladies had dabbled in astrology, but Nancy was reported to arrange the president's schedule according to her personal astrologer's advice.

★ ★ ★ ★ ★ ★ ★ ★ ★ ★

Women Break Through

1981 Sandra Day O'Connor is the first woman appointed to the U.S. Supreme Court.

1981 Jeane Kirkpatrick becomes the first female U.S. ambassador to the United Nations.

1981 The Supreme Court overturns state laws designating a husband "head and master" with sole control of property owned jointly with his wife.

1984 Geraldine Ferraro becomes the first woman nominated for vice president by a major party.

1985 Wilma Mankiller is elected first female chief of an American Indian nation, the Cherokees.

1989 Ileana Ros-Lehtinen of Florida is the first Hispanic woman elected to Congress.

Openly affectionate, the Reagans watched the news at night together while eating on TV trays, or else ate out at fancy restaurants. They spent their weekends riding horses and watching old movies at Camp David.

She was fussy about the people around him, making sure they had his best interests at heart while he tried to stimulate economic growth, cut government spending, and end the Cold War with the Soviet Union.

She was also fussy about her stuff. She had the staff label her clothes with the purchase dates and when the item was last worn. With tons of knickknacks, like twenty hand-painted porcelain boxes, she was furious if she found them out of place or—even worse—broken. Before state dinners she would have rehearsals so she could sample every course and even arrange the food on the platters herself—no "gray food," only bright colors.

★ ★ ★ ★ ★ ★ ★ ★ ★ ★ ★ ★ ★

Graceful Under Pressure

Once after Nancy stood up and her skirt fell down to her feet, she said to her visitor, "I guess this is one meeting you'll never forget." After a concert, when her chair slipped off the stage and hurled her into a row of chrysanthemums, she assured everyone she was fine: "I just wanted to liven things up."

★ ★ ★ ★ ★ ★ ★ ★ ★ ★ ★ ★ ★

She often gave her husband advice—sometimes he took it and sometimes he didn't, as when she urged him to speak up about the AIDS crisis long before he eventually did. A breast cancer survivor, she spoke openly about her own mastectomy, encouraging other women to take care of their health, as Betty Ford had.

She took as her cause the fight against drug and alcohol abuse among young people. After researching the issue, she came up with the Just Say No campaign, urging kids to take responsibility for their own actions. To some the campaign seemed simplistic, but it was popular and she was passionate: "If it saves one child's life, it's worth it."

Five years after they left office, they disclosed that Ronald had Alzheimer's disease. For the next ten years, she was his primary caretaker. After he died of the disease, she grew more active in politics, speaking out about various candidates, and giving advice to Michelle Obama.

She also took up the cause of stem cell research. It was controversial, but she lobbied the next presidents to fund it, believing it could lead to a cure for Alzheimer's and other diseases. She cheered Barack Obama when he finally reversed the ban on funding in 2009.

Nancy died at age ninety-four of congestive heart failure.

Barbara Bush (served from 1989–1993)

Barbara Bush (1925–) couldn't remember a time when she didn't love to read. Her father was the publisher of two popular women's magazines, *Redbook* and *McCall's*, and in the evenings her family would gather, each absorbed in different reading material.

She was sixteen when she met George H. W. Bush, and they got engaged a year and a half later, just before he went off to serve in World War II as a navy torpedo bomber pilot. By the time George returned on leave, Barbara had dropped out of Smith College, wanting to devote herself to her marriage and family.

In their first forty-four years of marriage, raising six children, Barbara managed twenty-nine moves, thanks to George's careers in the navy, the oil business, and various positions in government. Her son George W. described her as a parental powerhouse: "My mother's always been a very outspoken person who vents very well—she'll just let rip if she's got something on her mind." With her husband frequently out of town, she earned the nickname "the Enforcer."

The death of her three-year-old daughter Robin from leukemia left her with a deep well of compassion. It was then that her hair turned from brown to white. "Because of Robin," she said, "George and I love every living human more."

At times Barbara felt isolated—when George was gone or when his jobs were top secret and he wasn't allowed to talk about his work. She suffered a spell of depression, which deepened as she noticed that younger women were increasingly achieving their own goals rather than helping with their husbands'.

She started carving out more of her own space,

giving speeches with a slide show about her year living in China, volunteering at a hospice, speaking about getting the Equal Rights Amendment ratified and her agreement with the Supreme Court's decision on the rights of women to terminate their pregnancies. Possibly after her son Neil's diagnosis as dyslexic, she became passionate about reading and literacy issues.

WOMEN BREAK THROUGH
1993 Women are allowed to wear pants on the U.S. Senate floor.

In the White House, Barbara mostly avoided speaking directly about politics as her husband tried to improve the economy, urging citizens to become "a thousand points of light" in solving the country's problems. Abroad, he launched the Gulf War in Iraq and dealt with the Soviet Union as it fell apart.

As her special cause she chose literacy, founding the Barbara Bush Foundation for Family Literacy. She insisted that working for a more literate America was the "most important issue we have," and cast her net wide to create a national network of support. She wrote books about her dogs and donated the profits to literacy groups. A strong advocate of volunteerism, she also helped other causes—including the homeless, AIDS, the elderly, and school volunteer programs.

Barbara had a warm, grandmotherly image that people liked. They admired her white hair—she was known as the Silver Fox—and her signature three strands of fake pearls. The staff adored her. She never made special requests or took herself too seriously, basically letting the cooks make whatever they wanted and genuinely appreciating it. Because she hated it when people sang happy birthday to her, the staff would make her a little cake with the musical notes for the song in the frosting, letting her enjoy a book while she ate it by herself.

Barbara's Big Speech

When she was asked to speak at Wellesley College in Massachusetts in 1990, some of the female students objected. Many felt she had defined herself through the person she married rather than as an individual. Barbara spoke anyway, a serious speech about the conflict unique to women, the desire to have both a family and a career. The students ended up appreciating her gracious analysis of a changing world. And her humor helped—she finished by hoping that one of the males in the audience might one day follow in her footsteps as a helpmate to a president—"and I wish *him* well!"

With the 2001 election of her son George W. Bush as president, Barbara became the only other woman besides Abigail Adams to be both the wife and mother of U.S. presidents. Another one of her sons is Florida's former governor, Jeb Bush.

Barbara divides her time between her home in Houston, Texas, and the family summer home in Kennebunkport, Maine, keeping up with her children and grandchildren. She serves on the boards of AmeriCares and the Mayo Clinic, and is honorary chair of the Barbara Bush Foundation—with plenty of time to read.

CHAPTER 17

Developing a Thick Skin

Hillary Clinton

Hillary Clinton (served from 1993–2001)

Hillary Clinton (1947-) has held paying jobs ever since she was thirteen. The messiest ones were when she worked her way across Alaska by washing dishes in Mount McKinley National Park and sliming salmon in a fish processing cannery—but this was how she helped to pay her college and law school costs.

From an early age, her goal was to find a job where she could serve her country and help people the most.

She put herself on the map at her college graduation, when she gave a rousing speech that had everyone standing and clapping: "The challenge now is to practice politics as the art of making what appears to be impossible, possible."

She was named one of the brightest student leaders in America and appeared on TV talk shows. Now that more women were entering politics, people were starting to see a political future for her. As early as 1972 some were beginning to speak about her becoming the first woman president.

One day at law school, she went up to Bill Clinton and said, "If you're going to keep staring at me, I might as well introduce myself." They had many big ideas in common, and she liked that he wasn't afraid of her, as many men were. He said later that he thought she was "the most gifted person I'd ever met" and "I'd rather spend the night talking to her than anybody I can think of."

Trying to serve her country, she reported that she tried to join the marines in 1975. They turned her down, she said, claiming, "You're too old, you can't see, and you're a woman."

It was as a lawyer and law professor that she advanced.

Her reputation was such that she was asked to join the committee investigating criminal charges against Richard Nixon, one of three women on the team. When the group's findings forced him to resign in 1974, the only president to leave office in disgrace, she went into history books along with the rest of her team.

For years she supported and guided Bill's career: "Whenever I had trouble, she was a rock in our family," he said. "I trust her with my life, and have on more than one occasion." While raising her daughter, Chelsea, she was a partner in a law firm and the breadwinner in the family.

Then she worked eighteen-hour days to get Bill elected president. She became the first First Lady to have a highly successful career of her own and to hold advanced degrees.

HOMEWORK FOR BEING A FIRST LADY

Hillary prepared for the job by reading forty-three biographies of other First Ladies. She admired several, and aimed for a combination of gracious Dolley Madison and social justice activist Eleanor Roosevelt. She always kept a portrait of Eleanor in her office, and on her toughest days asked herself, "What would Eleanor do?"

During their administration, Bill tried to present it as a "two for one" deal—the country would benefit from Hillary's expertise and vision. But she ran into barriers other First Ladies had—she wasn't an elected official, and many didn't see how she should be allowed to make policy.

HILLARY HATRED

As many fans as Hillary has—in 2014 she was named the most admired woman in the world—she has many who despise her. They call her ugly names, spread weird rumors, criticize her looks (especially her hair), sell insulting merchandise, and attack her whenever possible. She followed Eleanor Roosevelt in developing a thick skin and positive attitude: "Take criticism seriously but not personally," she told herself. "If there is truth or merit in the criticism, try to learn from it. Otherwise, let it roll right off you."

One of the country's biggest crises was insurance for health care—thirty-seven million adults and children were going without it. Bill appointed her to chair the Task Force on National Health Care Reform, overseeing the work of five hundred people to solve the problem. She introduced major legislation to Congress (the first First Lady to do so) that would have provided health care for every American. It failed, possibly because of mistakes she made, or because many were violently opposed to a First Lady making policy; she had to wear a bulletproof vest while campaigning for it. (Not until 2010 did Barack Obama succeed in getting similar legislation passed.)

While Bill oversaw a long period of peace and economic expansion, she stayed busy, writing books and a weekly newspaper column, surrounded by a large collection of frog figurines inspired by a private joke with Bill. Traveling on behalf of women's rights, she began winning admirers for shedding light on conditions for women and girls around the world. She denounced abusive practices—such as the treatment of women in Afghanistan by Islamic fundamentalists—and called for empowering women as the best way to make a country more stable.

Whenever Chelsea was free for a meal, Hillary would rearrange her schedule—Chelsea was her first priority. When Chelsea was sick, she made comfort foods like scrambled eggs and apple sauce herself. Later she asked the chef to teach Chelsea how to cook, wanting her to be self-sufficient.

WOMEN BREAK THROUGH

1993 Janet Reno is the first woman attorney general of the United States.

1997 Madeleine Albright becomes the first woman U.S. secretary of state.

Of all her problems as First Lady, the most painful was making the choice to stay with Bill after his affair with a White House intern was revealed to the public. The staff could overhear them having big fights. During the darkest days of the scandal, when he became the second president to be impeached (and then acquitted of wrongdoing), she arranged with the staff to hang out at the pool for hours by herself, and she ordered her favorite dessert, mocha cake, almost every night. Many supported her choice to stay, and many didn't.

"The most difficult decisions I have made in my life were to stay married to Bill and to run for the Senate from New York," she wrote. Before their White House time was even over, she took a deep breath and ran for office on her own. In 2000 she was elected to the Senate, the first First Lady elected to the Senate and the first woman elected statewide in New York.

★ ★ ★ ★ ★ ★ ★ ★ ★ ★ ★ ★ ★ ★

BILL'S TURN

After the White House, it was Bill's turn to support her. "We were married a very long time when she was always, in effect, deferring to my political career," he said. "I told her when she got elected to the Senate from New York that she'd given me twenty-six years, and so I intended to give her twenty-six years. Whatever she wanted to do was fine with me. If she wanted to know my opinion, I would tell her, but she had carte blanche to make whatever decisions she wanted, and tell me what I was supposed to do about it."

★ ★ ★ ★ ★ ★ ★ ★ ★ ★ ★ ★ ★ ★

On September 11, 2001, after the al-Qaeda attacks, she was on one of the few planes flying in the sky later that day, speeding to the New York City disaster scene and finding out what everybody needed. Two years later, in the Senate, she voted for invading Iraq, a vote she later called a mistake.

In 2008 Hillary made the daring move to run for president on her own, but was defeated for the nomination by Barack Obama. As president, he asked her to serve as his secretary of state, a crucial leadership post representing his foreign policy around the world. She turned it down the first few times he asked—but it certainly was a way to make a difference. She probably also noticed that it put her fourth in line to the presidency (after the president, vice president, and the speaker of the

House of Representatives). After a week of debating with herself and seeking advice, she accepted: "When your president asks you to serve, you should say yes."

Her favorite gift in her new job was a teddy bear that sang "Don't worry, be happy." The job was never ending—building new partnerships and repairing ones that were strained, keeping the president advised, overseeing the work of the thousands of people in the department. As the most traveled secretary of state in history, she was rarely in her office, but in the air, fighting jet lag, grabbing meals on the run.

She made women's rights central to foreign policy, creating a new position—ambassador-at-large for Global Women's Issues. She also launched the Women in Public Service Project, with the lofty goal of women having equal representation in worldwide government jobs by 2050.

★   ★   ★

HILLARY ON WOMEN

- "Women are too often erased from our nation's history" (a 2015 reaction to news that the Treasury Department is going to put a woman on the ten-dollar bill).
- "If women are healthy and educated, their families will flourish. . . . And when families flourish, communities and nations will flourish" (in her historic 1995 speech in China at the United Nations Fourth World Conference on Women).
- "It is no longer acceptable to discuss women's rights as separate from human rights" (from the same speech).

- "I'm a big believer in women making the choices that are right for them" (a 1992 response to reporters questioning her decision to have a career and not to "stay home and bake cookies").
- "Becoming a grandmother has made me think deeply about the responsibility we all share as stewards of the world we inherit and will one day pass on" (from her 2014 book, *Hard Choices*).

★　　★　　★

She believed it was important to establish goodwill even in areas hostile to Americans. Her most controversial moment came in 2012, when she accepted responsibility for security lapses after Islamic militants attacked the American military compound in Benghazi, Libya, and killed four Americans.

"I am working so much harder now than I ever have in my entire life," she said. After four years on the job—and twenty years in public office—she took a break to be a private citizen. She gave speeches, wrote a book, and started more projects fostering improvement for women and girls.

According to a 2014 poll of historians and scholars, Hillary is the First Lady easiest to imagine serving as president.

CHAPTER 18

The Bookworm

Laura Bush

Laura Bush (served from 2001–2009)

Were it not for 9/11, the journey of Laura Bush (1946–) as First Lady might have been quite different.

She had tried various jobs—"I was determined to settle on a job, and I wanted to be surrounded by books."

When young she followed current events—supporting the civil rights movement, distraught over JFK's assassination—but wasn't especially political.

While getting her college degree in education, she assumed she'd find a husband in college, but it didn't happen. For her graduation gift she went on a tour of Europe with family, visiting ten countries. She joined a women's consciousness-raising group and read the classics of feminism by Betty Friedan and Germaine Greer.

She applied for a job with her local congressman in Washington, but when she refused to learn how to type—"in a burst of intellectual snobbery and a bit of feminism"—she naturally didn't get the job.

At seventeen she'd been involved in a car accident, and she didn't like to drive after that. She turned down two teaching jobs at schools that were too far away to walk to, finally accepting one that was on her street. She worked for several years as an elementary school teacher and librarian, going back to school to get her master's degree in library science. Teaching primarily African American and Latino students, where she felt she could have the most impact, she discovered the thrill of story time: sharing library books with kids was her passion.

In 1977 friends fixed her up with George W. Bush (who had once dated Pat Nixon's daughter Tricia), son of future President George H. W. Bush. At first she wasn't enthused because his family was so political, and she wasn't that interested. In a large gathering of intimidating Bushes, when asked what *she* did, she reportedly said, "I read, I smoke, I admire." She was her own person, mellow and mysterious.

But George made her laugh, he proposed after six weeks, and he turned out to be a wonderful dad to their twin daughters, Jenna and Barbara. Later, when he dealt with a drinking problem, she gave him her support—"I let him know that I thought he could be a better man"—and he quit.

When he became governor of Texas, she put all her energy into the Texas Department of Family and Protective Services, wanting to save children from abuse and neglect. She also founded the Texas Book Festival, a major annual event, in 1995 to inspire people of all ages to love reading.

Bookish Laura Facts
- She organizes all her books by the Dewey decimal system.
- Much more interested in new books than new recipes, she hosted only four formal state dinners at the White House and preferred informal barbecues.
- She spent evenings reading with George, going to bed early.

Once in the White House, she told the staff, "I'm not here for me, I'm here for George. Whatever I do here is to help the president's goals for the country." And yet she did have her own interests: education and early childhood development.

Her first deed as First Lady was to throw a party for her favorite writers: "Our country's authors have helped forge the American identity, create its memory, and define and reinforce our national consciousness."

She began work on a large number of projects. Most famous was establishing and organizing the National Book Festival in Washington in 2001, an ongoing literary extravaganza that introduces as many as two hundred thousand people to their favorite authors each year.

On the morning of September 11, 2001, she was on her way to brief a Senate committee about a conference she'd organized when she learned about the terrorist attacks on America. Much of her attention afterward was diverted to the war on terror, and she fully supported her husband's actions in dealing with the crisis. Her first concern was for the young: "Don't let your children see the images" of the falling World Trade Center towers being replayed on TV. She suggested reading them a story instead.

She kept going with her issues—education and the well-being of women and families worldwide. She was a key advocate of George's education reform—the No Child Left Behind Act—and a supporter of the Reading First program, the largest early reading initiative in American history. She launched Ready to Read, Ready to Learn, which promoted the best practices in early education and highlighted the best teacher training programs. She hosted the first-ever White House Conference on Global Literacy in 2006.

★   ★   ★

BEING FIRST LADY

- "First Ladies, whether giving 'silly speeches' [as Mary Lincoln was accused of] or serving as the president's adviser, have made and changed history" (during a speech at the First Ladies Library. Her personal role model was her mother-in-law, Barbara Bush).
- "For the first time, I realized the degree to which I had a unique forum as First Lady. People would pay attention to what I said. I had always known that intellectually, but now I realized it emotionally" (after receiving an emotional thank-you from women in Afghanistan).
- Arguing that First Ladies should be able to keep up their careers: "Certainly a first gentleman might continue to work at whatever he did."

★   ★   ★

She met with students in seventy-five countries, encouraging girls and women to pursue education. She spoke out against the Taliban's oppression of women and children in Afghanistan, journeyed there three times, and served as honorary chair of the U.S.–Afghan Women's Council. She made five trips to Africa alone in support of global health initiatives—AIDS relief and eradicating malaria.

★   ★   ★

WISE WORDS

In Jordan, at the World Economic Forum in 2005, Laura spoke out for women: "In my country women didn't secure the right to vote until more than a century after our nation's founding. But now we know that a nation can only achieve its best future and its brightest potential when all of its citizens, men and women, participate in the government and in decision-making." At that point, the entire delegation from Saudi Arabia (where women can't drive, much less vote) got up and walked out in protest.

★   ★   ★

At times the war on terror and in Iraq affected her plans. When she scheduled a salon with poets and then learned that all of them opposed the war in Iraq, she simply canceled it. When the government, in search of terrorists, started investigating library records and freedom to read seemed threatened, she said, "We are in a special time right now, where we need to do everything we can to avoid another attack."

In retirement, back in Texas, she has worked on projects with Michelle Obama and Hillary Clinton. Not always in line with her husband's views, she has felt free to speak out that same-sex marriage should be legal, abortion should be kept legal, and men and women should have income equality. In 2015, she announced an ambitious program to stop the decline of the monarch butterfly population.

Meanwhile, she created the Laura Bush Foundation for America's Libraries, which every year awards grants totaling one million dollars to school libraries.

On Doing More

In 2014, a poll of scholars and experts ranked Laura Bush as the First Lady who could have done more with her time at the White House. They judged, perhaps unfairly, that she mostly played it safe by focusing on literacy instead of matters that were more life-and-death and historically significant. She was followed by Pat Nixon, Mamie Eisenhower, Bess Truman, and Barbara Bush.

CHAPTER 19

Serious Role Model

Michelle Obama

Michelle Obama (served from 2009–2016)

The parents of her first roommate at Princeton University demanded a room change. They didn't want their white daughter living with a black girl.

As our first African American First Lady, Michelle Obama (1964-) has coped with double challenges to her role as a powerful woman. How did she prevail?

Her parents were always there for her and her brother. The family did most things together. Michelle looked forward to family dinners every night—except Wednesday, which was "the sad and unfortunate" liver night: "My father loved liver, and it just depressed me and my brother to no end when we knew it was liver time."

Except for liver, her parents couldn't have been more supportive, constantly emphasizing hard work, good judgment, and self-discipline, telling them not to be followers and not to be afraid of failure but instead learn from it. Michelle grew up as someone who "really does hate to lose," said her brother.

Michelle took piano lessons and drama classes, hitting speed bumps during her years in Chicago public schools: "Kids teasing me when I studied hard. Teachers telling me not to reach too high because my test scores weren't good enough. Folks making it clear . . . that success wasn't meant for a little girl like me."

Still, she forged ahead and made it to Princeton University, studying sociology and African American studies. She struggled at first with basic college skills, but watched how other students handled the problem— by getting help—and found a wise adviser and older students to mentor her.

After graduating from Harvard Law School

(becoming the third First Lady with a postgraduate degree), she joined a Chicago law firm. There she later met Barack Obama—she was his boss, actually. She was making a lot of money, driving a Mercedes-Benz, when the death of her father hit her hard: "If I die tomorrow, what did I really do with my life? What kind of a mark would I leave?"

★   ★   ★

WISE WORDS

- "Maybe you feel like your destiny was written the day you were born and you ought to just rein in your hopes and scale back your dreams. But if any of you are thinking that way, I'm here to tell you: *Stop it*" (in a 2010 speech to graduating high school seniors).
- "If you want to have a say in your community, if you truly want the power to control your own destiny, then you've got to be involved. You got to be at the table. You've got to vote, vote, vote, vote. That's it; that's the way we move forward. That's how we make progress for ourselves and for our country" (in a 2015 commencement address at Tuskegee University).
- "All of this [racism] used to really get to me. . . . I had to ignore all of the noise and be true to myself—and the rest would work itself out. I have learned that as long as I hold fast to my beliefs and values—and follow my own moral compass—then the only expectations I need to live up to are my own" (from the Tuskegee speech).

★   ★   ★

She changed gears, working in the Chicago city government to encourage people to serve their communities and their neighbors. She found the most fulfillment as the founding director of the Chicago chapter of Public Allies, a program that prepares young people for public service. She worked there almost four years, raising record-breaking amounts for the organization, constantly stretching herself: "I was never happier in my life than when I was working to build Public Allies."

Married to Barack in 1992, she was working at University of Chicago Hospitals as vice president for Community and External Affairs, bringing campus and community together, when her husband's political career took off.

Her life was already a juggling act, also raising her daughters, Sasha and Malia, while Barack was away campaigning. She often nagged him to help out more, to put the butter back, or put his own socks into the hamper.

With two small kids and a full-time job she loved, she had to be talked into his presidential campaign. She made a deal that he had to stop smoking, a promise he had difficulty keeping.

Michelle cut back on her job and spent more and more time campaigning for him. She turned out to be so good at it that some wondered if she should be the one who was the candidate.

Her most controversial moment came when she expressed gratitude at the public's positive response to a black candidate: "For the first time in my adult life, I am proud of my country because it feels like hope is making a comeback." It wasn't meant as antipatriotic, but as an earnest observation from an African American whose great-great-grandfather was a slave, who recalled "the folks who crossed the street in fear of their safety; the clerks who kept a close eye on us in all those department stores; the people at formal events who assumed we were the help."

The White House Now

The mansion has improved over the years. Today it has 132 rooms, 28 fireplaces, 8 staircases, 3 elevators, and solar panels on the roof. It's set on 18 acres of land, taken care of by two dozen National Park Service staff, in downtown Washington. The staff of 95 full-time employees and many more part-time workers keep it all running. Perks include an indoor heated pool, a beauty parlor, a pastry shop, a flower shop, and a private movie theater.

Once in the White House, having just finished off paying student loans, the two were unused to being taken care of so well. On their first night there, after all the inauguration balls were over, they were found dancing by themselves to a Mary J. Blige song.

She consulted with at least four former First Ladies about how to chart her path, though she was already determined that it would be family oriented. She considered being mom in chief her top priority, and she had *rules*. Family dinners, from which boxed macaroni and cheese was banned, were the most important part of the day. Sasha and Malia had to do their own chores (like laundry) and had to take up two sports. They were not allowed to have cell phones until they were twelve, and no Facebook until they were seventeen.

She planted a garden, the largest White House garden ever, and tried to make it the source for their meals. She hosted the ultimate sleepover for Girl Scouts with fifty fourth graders, with NASA scientists and astronauts available to watch the stars with them.

A 2014 poll named Michelle as the First Lady who most effectively managed family life while in office.

Besides mom in chief, she was also known as hugger in chief. She hugs a lot, more than most First Ladies: "I've always been a big hugger—that's just how I am—and it's always my first instinct when I meet someone."

She was one of Barack's most important advisers behind the scenes. Ahead of him on supporting gay marriage, she started speaking for equality early on.

★ ★ ★ ★ ★ ★ ★ ★ ★ ★ ★ ★ ★

MICHELLE ON FIRST LADIES

- Like other First Ladies, she worried about how she would keep her own identity: "WHAT IS TO BECOME OF ME?" she wrote in her journal when Barack wanted to run for president. She thought it through and decided it could work: "It took me a while to get out of my own head, and to set aside my own fears and self-interest, and focus on all the good that I believed a man like my husband could do as president."
- She once heard the job of First Lady referred to as "the balance between politics and sanity," and she agreed. "I have a huge responsibility to use this platform in a way that's going to make a difference."

★ ★ ★ ★ ★ ★ ★ ★ ★ ★ ★ ★ ★

Women Break Through

2015 According to a poll, 92 percent of Americans say they'd be willing to vote for a woman for president—up from 33 percent in 1937.

2016 The Treasury Department announces that African American abolitionist and spy Harriet Tubman will replace Andrew Jackson on the twenty dollar bill.

Michelle also launched four programs of her own: Let's Move! had a goal of ending the epidemic of childhood obesity within a generation. Joining Forces called on Americans to support service members, veterans, and their families through wellness, education, and employment opportunities. The Reach Higher initiative inspired young Americans to complete their education past high school and take charge of their future. Let Girls Learn called on countries around the world to do more to educate and empower young women.

Reaching Up

In at least one way, Michelle towered over almost every First Lady of the past. She is the tallest—joining Eleanor Roosevelt at five feet eleven inches.

After the White House, she looked forward to writing her memoirs, staying fit, traveling to beautiful places, being a grandmother someday—and probably a lot more.

CHAPTER 20

Glamour to Spare

Melania Trump (served from 2017–)

Melania Trump (1970-) is not your traditional First Lady. As well as being the wealthiest, she is the only one who is the president's third wife. She is the only one to have marketed her own brands of jewelry and skin-care products. She is the first First Lady to be born in a communist nation, Yugoslavia, and only the second to be born abroad, after Louisa Adams. She is the first First Lady whose native language is not English. She speaks five languages—as did Lou Hoover and Jacqueline Kennedy—hers are Slovenian, Serbian, English, French, and German.

She's also the first to have been a supermodel. First Ladies like Pat Nixon and Betty Ford worked as models, but Melania is the only one to have had a successful career and also the only one who posed nude. At five feet eleven, she is tied with Michelle Obama and Eleanor Roosevelt for tallest First Lady.

She grew up in the small hilly town of Sevnica, Slovenia, known then for its medieval castle and annual salami festival. She lived in a housing block for the government-owned textile factory, where her mother worked. While wrapping her notebooks in perfume ads from magazines, making bracelets in art class, and exchanging boy-crazy notes with friends along the lines of yarn strung between their apartment balconies, she had big dreams.

At sixteen she caught the attention of fashion photographers, and after one year at college studying architecture, she dropped out to focus on modeling. Her big break was winning second-place in a magazine's "Slovenian Face of the Year" contest, which put her on a track to Milan, Paris, and New York, modeling for top magazines and major stores. She met billionaire businessman Donald J. Trump, 24 years older than she, at a party at New York's Kit Kat Club.

Said Donald: "We literally have never had an argument.... We just are very compatible."

Their wedding, which made her stepmom to his four children from two previous marriages, was full of celebrities, including Bill and Hillary Clinton. The wedding cake was a fifty-pound orange Grand Marnier chocolate truffle cake created by their private chef and covered with 3,000 roses.

She plans to be a "very traditional" First Lady—like Betty Ford or Jackie Kennedy. She is active in charities that support women and children. Her highest priority is parenting their son, Barron: "I am a full-time mom; that is my first job." Now eleven, Barron likes to wear suits and ties and wants to be just like his father, a businessman and a golfer. "I call him mini-Donald," says Melania.

"I chose not to go into politics and policy," she has said. "Those policies are my husband's job."

At the same time, she has her own views: "I follow the news from A to Z and I know what's going on.... I give

MELANIA ON IMMIGRATION

Some find it ironic that, considering Trump's opposition to migrants, Melania is herself an immigrant. "I follow the law," she insisted. "On July 28th, 2006, I was very proud to become a citizen of the United States—the greatest privilege on planet Earth. I cannot, or will not, take the freedoms this country offers for granted."

him my opinions many, many times."

Melania admits that she doesn't always agree with everything that her husband says, but sees this as "normal" in a marriage: "I'm standing very strong on the ground on my two feet and I'm my own person. And I think that's very important in the relationship."

When it comes time to pick a cause as First Lady, she says, "I will choose what is dearest to my heart and work on that a hundred percent. . . . I will use that wonderful privilege to try to help people in our country who need it the most."

Traditional or not, Melania is bound to make her mark with glamour and style.

CHAPTER 21

Forty Women Who Shaped America

It's small wonder that many of our First Ladies were more popular than their husbands—these are amazing, proactive, accomplished women, especially considering the way society tried to keep them cooped up. Among other feats, each woman kept her mate grounded and in many cases she was the only human being he could be himself around.

All have had immense challenges. All have dealt with them in direct or indirect ways, some of them publicly and famously.

Many haven't been properly researched yet, with scholars traditionally tending to focus on men. For some, information is scant. As more scholarship comes out, their contributions may be even greater than we thought.

★ ★ ★ ★ ★ ★ ★ ★ ★ ★ ★ ★ ★ ★ ★

THE BEST PLACE FOR MORE FACTS,
INCLUDING WHAT YOU NEED FOR REPORTS
National First Ladies' Library, www.firstladies.org

★ ★ ★ ★ ★ ★ ★ ★ ★ ★ ★ ★ ★ ★ ★

In the future, First Ladies are always going to be of the highest possible interest. A man's choice of mate says a lot about him—part of being president is picking a worthy First Lady. (Notice how many presidents married *up*—women with more education or wealth than them.)

The ones so far have enhanced our country in many resplendent ways. As Hillary Clinton put it, "Whoever is part of the family of a president has an extraordinary privilege of not only having a front-row seat on history but making her or maybe his contribution."

Through all the dramatic twists and turns of the American story, First Ladies have been there—coming to the rescue, rising to the occasion, making sacrifices, serving their country.

Selected Sources

Allgor, Catherine. *A Perfect Union: Dolley Madison and the Creation of the American Nation*. New York: Henry Holt, 2006.

Beasley, Maurine H. *Eleanor Roosevelt: Transformative First Lady*. Lawrence: University Press of Kansas, 2010.

Boller, Paul F., Jr. *Presidential Wives: An Anecdotal History*. 2nd rev. ed. New York: Oxford University Press, 1998.

Brady, Patricia. *Martha Washington: An American Life*. New York: Viking, 2005.

Brower, Kate Andersen. *The Residence: Inside the Private World of the White House*. New York: HarperCollins, 2015.

Bush, Laura. *Spoken from the Heart*. New York: Scribner, 2010.

Clinton, Catherine. *Mrs. Lincoln: A Life*. New York: Harper Perennial, 2010.

Clinton, Hillary. *Hard Choices*. New York: Simon & Schuster, 2014.

First Ladies: Influence and Image. C-SPAN. http://firstladies.c-span.org.

First Ladies Library Blog. http://www.firstladies.org/blog/.

Jacobs, Diane. *Dear Abigail: The Intimate Lives and Revolutionary Ideas of Abigail Adams and Her Two Remarkable Sisters*. New York: Ballantine Books, 2014.

Krull, Kathleen. *Lives of the Presidents: Fame, Shame (and What the Neighbors Thought)*. Boston: HMH Books for Young Readers, 2011.

Landau, Barry H. *The President's Table: Two Hundred Years of Dining and Diplomacy*. New York: HarperCollins, 2007.

Leaming, Barbara. *Jacqueline Bouvier Kennedy Onassis: The Untold Story*. New York: St. Martin's Press, 2014.

Martha Washington: A Life. http://marthawashington.us.

Mayo, Edith P., ed. *The Smithsonian Book of the First Ladies: Their Lives, Times, and Issues*. New York: Henry Holt, 1996.

Miller, Kristie. *Ellen and Edith: Woodrow Wilson's First Ladies.* Lawrence: University Press of Kansas, 2010.

National First Ladies' Library. http://www.firstladies.org.

National Women's History Museum. https://www.nwhm.org.

O'Brien, Cormac. *Secret Lives of the First Ladies: What Your Teachers Never Told You about the Women of the White House.* Philadelphia, PA: Quirk, 2009.

Pinkpillbox (Jacqueline Kennedy site). http://www.pinkpillbox. com.

Roberts, John B., II. *Rating the First Ladies: The Women Who Influenced the Presidency.* New York: Citadel Press, 2003.

Siena College Research Institute/C-SPAN. First Ladies Study. http://webdev.siena.edu/centers-institutes/siena-research-institute/social-cultural-polls/first-ladies-study/.

Slevin, Peter. *Michelle Obama: A Life.* New York: Knopf, 2015.

Swain, Susan, and C-SPAN. *First Ladies: Presidential Historians on the Lives of 45 Iconic American Women.* New York: PublicAffairs, 2015.

The First Ladies. The White House. https://www.whitehouse. gov/1600/first-ladies.

Truman, Margaret. *First Ladies.* New York: Random House, 1995.

INDEX

Adams, Abigail
  critique from, 15–16
  letter writing of, 21–23, 27
  as mother, 46
  as "Mrs. President," 26
  portraits of, 19–20
  relationship of, 21–22
  role models for, 26
  service of, 20
  slavery views of, 22
  during wartime, 24
Adams, John
  history of, 21
  as minister, 24
  relationship of, 21–22
Adams, John Quincy
  presidency of, 26
  promise of, 22
  son of, 46
Adams, Louisa
  depression of, 47–48
  popularity of, 46–47
  portrait of, 41
  service of, 45
  slavery views of, 47–48
  as writer, 47
Albright, Madeleine, 208
Alcott, Louisa May, 86
Alley Bill, 121
American Revolution
  allies during, 44
  DAR, 105, 146
  first lady during, 4
  letter writing during, 27
  Washington, M., during, 12–13
Anderson, Marian, 146, 159
Antioch College, 66
Anti-Slavery Society, 48
Arkansas, 139
Arthur, Chester A., 32

Betty Ford Center, 186
Bill of Rights, 126

birth control, 119
Black Brain Trust, 147
Black Cabinet, 147
Blackwell, Elizabeth, 60
Buchanan, James, 31
Bush, Barbara
  as "the enforcer," 199
  literacy advocacy of, 200–201
  portraits of, 187, 198
  retirement of, 200–201
  speech of, 200
Bush, George H. W., 199
Bush, George W.
  dating of, 215
  drinking of, 216
  education reform of, 217
Bush, Laura
  early accomplishments of,
    215–16
  foundation of, 220
  interests of, 216–17
  portraits of, 213–14
  quotes from, 218
  role model of, 218
  views of, 219–20

Camelot, 169
Camp David, 160
Carter, Jimmy
  advice for, 190
  in office, 191
  views of, 191–92
Carter, Rosalynn
  accomplishments of, 191–92
  history of, 189
  political role of, 190
  portraits of, 187–88
  "steel magnolia," 189
  views of, 191
Carter Center, 191
Chao, Elaine, 217
Checkers speech, 179
Chisholm, Shirley, 175

civil rights
  Kennedy, Jacqueline,
    supporting, 166
  lawyers for, 147
  Parks, R., arrest, 159
  Roosevelt advocating, 147
  Title VII of, 175
Civil War
  break out of, 76
  Grant, U., in, 89
  hero, 108
  Lincoln, A., in, 76–77
  nurse in, 86
  Polk, S., during, 61
  recovery from, 93
Clarke School for the Deaf, 134
Cleveland, Frances
  popularity of, 102–3
  portrait of, 99
  service of, 100, 101
  suffrage views of, 103
Cleveland, Grover
  death of, 103
  presidency of, 101–2
Clinton, Bill
  after affair, 208
  during election, 206
  as husband, 209
  presidency of, 207
Clinton, Chelsea
  childhood of, 208
  duties of, 32
  during father's election, 206
Clinton, Hilary
  accomplishments of, 210–11
  early career of, 205
  on family, 237–38
  in health care reform, 207
  portraits of, 203–4
  role models of, 206
  as secretary of state, 209–10
  as Senator, 208–9
  views of, 207–8, 210–11
Code of Laws, 23

Committee for a More Beautiful
  Capital, 175
Continental Congress, 23
Coolidge, Calvin, 134–35
Coolidge, Grace
  after husband's death, 135–36
  interests of, 134
  portraits of, 127, 133
  rules for, 134–35
Crittenden House, 109
Cuban missile crisis, 167

Daughters of the American
  Revolution (DAR), 105, 146
Declaration of Independence, 23

Eisenhower, Dwight, 158
Eisenhower, Mamie
  death of, 161
  popularity of, 158–59
  portraits of, 151, 157
  relationship of, 160
Emancipation Proclamation, 85
"the Enforcer," 199
Equal Credit Opportunity Act, 181
Equal Employment Opportunity
  Commission, 186
Equal Pay Act, 167
Equal Rights Amendment, 131
Era of Good Feelings, 43

FDR. See Roosevelt, Franklin
  Delano
Ferraro, Geraldine, 195
Fillmore, Abigail
  death of, 66
  portraits of, 57, 64
  service of, 64, 65–66
Fillmore, Millard, 65
First Ladies
  during American Revolution, 4
  careers of, 3
  challenges of, 237
  criticism of, 5–6

duties of, 232
expectations of, 43
FLOTUS nickname for, 125
flying, 127
as hostesses, 6–7
job description of, 4–5
longest-lived, 156
president's with no, 29, 31–32
roles in, 238
sacrifices of, 238
secret service for, 125
supporting role of, 4–5
as teachers, 3
title of, 6
Ford, Betty
    career of, 184, 186
    portraits of, 171, 183
    views of, 185
Ford, Gerald, 184
Fourteenth Amendment, 87
French Revolution, 44
Friedan, Betty, 215

Garfield, James, 96–97
Garfield, Lucretia
    death of, 97
    portrait of, 95
    service of, 96
Girl Scouts
    first troop of, 116
    at funeral, 140
    Hoover, L., leading of, 140
    sleepover for, 227
Global Literacy, 218
Global Women's Issues, 210
governors, first female, 134
Grant, Julia
    death of, 91
    portrait of, 88
    service of, 88, 89
    views of, 90
Grant, Ulysses S.
    in Civil War, 89
    in Mexican-American war, 89

slavery views of, 90
Great Depression
    crisis of, 138–39
    government during, 140, 145
Greer, Germaine, 215
Guinea worm disease, 191–92

Habitat for Humanity, 192
Harding, Florence
    credit for, 130
    death of, 132
    favorite issues of, 131
    portrait of, 127
    service of, 128, 129
Harding, Warren, 129
Harrison, Anna
    career of, 50–51
    portraits of, 41, 49
    service of, 49–50
Harrison, Benjamin, 50
Harrison, Caroline
    death of, 106
    portraits of, 99, 104
    service of, 105–6
    words of, 105
Harrison, William Henry, 50
Hayes, Lucy
    history of, 93
    portrait of, 92
    as role model, 93
    views of, 94
Hayes, Rutherford, 93
Hickok, Lorena, 147
Highway Beautification Act, 175
homeless shelter, 109
Hoover, Herbert, 138–39
Hoover, Lou
    death of, 140
    interests of, 138
    joining League of Women
        Voters, 140
    portraits of, 127, 137
    staff relations of, 139
hospital, first women's, 68

income laws, 51
Indiana Territory, 50
Iraq, 219
"Iron Butterfly," 194

Jackson, Andrew, 31
Jackson, Mahalia, 159
Jefferson, Thomas, 31
JFK. See Kennedy, John F.
Johnson, Andrew
  enemies of, 86
  relationship of, 85–86
  slavery views of, 87
Johnson, Eliza
  health of, 85–86
  portrait of, 84
  slavery views of, 87
Johnson, Lady Bird
  accomplishments of, 175
  during campaign, 174
  career of, 173–76
  history of, 173
  portraits of, 171–72
Johnson, Lyndon
  during election, 174
  marriage proposal of, 173
  relationship of, 175–76
Jordan, 219
Junior Literary Guild, 149
Just Say No campaign, 197

Kennedy, Jacqueline
  accomplishments of, 167
  Camelot and, 169
  education of, 165
  family life of, 165–66
  after husband's death, 169
  portraits of, 163–64
  publishing career of, 169–70
  relationship of, 168
Kennedy, John F. (JFK)
  Cuban missile crisis, 167
  death of, 168
  on his wife, 167
  marriage of, 168
  presidency of, 165–66
Kennedy, Robert, 169
Kirkpatrick, Jeane, 195

laws
  Code of, 23
  income, 51
  about property, 51, 60, 90, 195
  about rape, 186
  for women, 23–24
lawyers
  civil rights, 147
  first female, 94
League of Women Voters
  foundation of, 123
  Hoover, L., joining of, 140
Let Girls Learn, 228
Let's Move!, 228
Lincoln, Abraham
  career of, 75–77
  in Civil War, 76–77
  death of, 79
Lincoln, Mary
  antislavery views of, 73, 77–78
  chores of, 75
  death of, 81
  mental issues of, 80
  portraits of, 71–72
  salary of, 77
Lincoln Bedroom, 79
Little Women (Alcott), 86
Lockwood, Belva Ann, 94
Low, Juliette Gordon, 116

Macaulay, Catharine, 26
Madison, Dolley
  apologies of, 39
  history of, 35
  honors of, 40
  as hostess, 36
  names of, 6
  portraits of, 33–34
  slavery and, 38
  snuff addiction of, 37

Madison, James, 35–36
Manifest Destiny, 60
Mankiller, Wilma, 195
Married Women's Property Act, 60
mayors, first female, 102
McCarthy, Joseph, 159
McKinley, Ida
  accomplishments of, 108
  history of, 108
  portraits of, 99, 107
  supporting voting rights, 109
McKinley, William
  accomplishments of, 108–9
  assassination of, 109
  as hero, 108
medical school
  first woman graduating from, 60
  money for, 8
mental health
  addiction treatment center for, 186
  advocacy for, 190–91
  Just Say No campaign for, 197
Mexican-American War
  climate after, 68
  Grant, U., in, 89
  hero of, 63
military, women in, 186
Mink, Patsy, 175
Mississippi, 51
monarch butterfly, 220
Monroe, Elizabeth
  death of, 44
  history of, 43
  interests of, 44
  portraits of, 41–42
Monroe, James
  foreign policy of, 44
  meeting of, 43
Monroe Doctrine, 44
Mott, Lucretia, 48, 60
"Mrs. President," 26
Ms. Magazine, 181

Murray, Pauli, 147

NAACP. See National Association for the Advancement of Colored People
National Amateur Athletic Federation, 140
National Association for the Advancement of Colored People (NAACP), 159
National Geographic Society, 176
National Health Care Reform, 207
National Organization for Women, 175
National Wildflower Research Center, 176
National Woman's Party, 123
National Women's Hall of Fame, 188
New Deal, 147
Nineteenth Amendment, 123–24
Nixon, Pat
  career of, 179–81
  coat of, 179
  history of, 178
  panda incident with, 180
  popularity of, 181
  portraits of, 171, 177
Nixon, Richard
  Checkers speech by, 179
  history of, 178
  resignation of, 181–82
  views of, 180–81
No Child Left Behind Act, 217

Obama, Barak, 225
Obama, Michelle
  career of, 225
  history of, 223
  as mom, 226–27
  portraits of, 221–22
  as role model, 221
  words of, 224
Oberlin College, 51
O'Connor, Sandra Day, 195

Office of Civilian Defense, 145
Oregon Territory, 60
Our Bodies, Ourselves, 181

Panama Canal, 112
pants, 200
Parks, Rosa, 159
Paul, Alice, 123
Pelosi, Nancy, 217
Perkins, Frances, 147
petticoat government, 125
Pierce, Franklin, 68–69
Pierce, Jane
    depression of, 68–69
    portraits of, 57, 67
Polk, James, 59
Polk, Sarah
    during Civil War, 61
    history of, 59
    portraits of, 57–58
    views of, 60
postage stamp, 111
Pregnancy Discrimination Act,
    190
Progressive Era, 112
property laws
    income laws, first laws for, 51
    married women's, 60
    sole ownership, 195
    in twenty three states, 90
Public Allies, 225

Quaker religion, 35

Rankin, Jeannette, 123
rape law, 186
Reach Higher initiative, 228
Reading First program, 217–18
Ready to Read, Ready to Learn,
    218
Reagan, Nancy
    interests of, 195
    as "Iron Butterfly," 194
    portraits of, 187, 193
    in theater, 194

views of, 196–97
Reagan, Ronald
    assassination attempt on, 195
    health of, 197
Red Cross, 109
Reno, Janet, 208
Rice, Condoleezza, 217
Richards, Ellen Swallow, 90
Roe v. Wade, 181
role models
    of Bush, L., 218
    Hayes, L., as, 93
    Obama, M., as, 221
Roosevelt, Edith
    death of, 112
    portrait of, 99, 110
    service of, 111
Roosevelt, Eleanor
    accomplishments of, 145–49
    as "best of the best," 148
    criticism of, 149
    history of, 143
    after husband's death, 148
    in later years, 150
    money and, 146
    portraits of, 141–42
    quotes of, 144
    relationships of, 147
Roosevelt, Franklin Delano (FDR)
    election of, 145
    marriage of, 143
    New Deal of, 146
    supporting suffrage, 144
Roosevelt, Theodore, 143
Ros-Lehtinen, Ileana, 195

Sanger, Margaret, 119
Secret Service, 125
Senate, 139
sexual harassment, 186
slavery
    Adams, A., view of, 22
    Adams, L., view of, 47–48
    Female Anti-Slavery Society, 48
    Grants, J., view of, 90

Johnson, E., view of, 87
Lincoln, M., view of, 73, 77–78
Madison, D., view of, 38
Tyler, J., campaigns for, 55–56
Washington, M. view of, 17
slippers, 109
Smith, Margaret Chase, 175
snuff, 37
Stanton, Elizabeth Cady, 60
"steel magnolia," 189
Stowe, Harriet Beecher, 55, 66
suffrage
   Cleveland, F., fighting for, 103
   FDR support of, 144
   Grant, J., fighting for, 90
   march for, 119
   start of, 78
   Wilson, Edith, against, 124

Taft, Helen
   portraits of, 99, 113
   service of, 113, 114
   views of, 115–16
Taft, William, 116
Taylor, Margaret
   portraits of, 57, 62
   service of, 62, 63
Taylor, Zachary, 63
Texas
   Book Festival, 216
   Bush, B., retired in, 201
   Department of Family and
      Protective Services, 216
   JFK assassination in, 168
   as state, 56
   University of, 173
Title IX of the Education
   Amendments, 181
Title VII of the Civil Rights Act,
   175
Truman, Bess
   career of, 154–55
   death of, 155–56
   history of, 153
   portraits of, 151–52

Truman, Harry, 153–54
Trump, Melania
   history of, 231
   on immigration, 232
   marriage of, 232
   portrait of, 229
Truth, Sojourner, 53
Tubman, Harriet, 66, 228
Twenty-fifth Amendment, 126
Tyler, John, 53
Tyler, Julia
   portraits of, 41, 54
   slavery campaigns of, 55–56
   Texas and, 56
Tyler, Letitia
   portraits of, 41, 52
   stroke of, 53

Uncle Tom's Cabin (Stowe), 55, 66
Universal Declaration of Human
   Rights, 149
U.S.-Afghan Women's Council, 218

Van Buren, Martin, 31
Vassar Female College, 76
Victorian Era, 43
Vietnam War, 166
*A Vindication of the Rights of
   Woman* (Wollstonecraft), 26
voters. *See* women voters

Warren, Mercy Otis, 26
Washington, George
   presidency of, 13–14
   qualities of, 12
   retirement of, 17–18
Washington, Martha
   during American Revolution,
      12–13
   clothing of, 15
   criticism of, 15–16
   heartbreak of, 12
   history of, 11
   as hostess, 14–15
   names of, 6

portraits of, 9–10
slavery views of, 17
on stamp, 111
words of, 16
Washington City Orphan Asylum, 39
Watergate scandal, 181
Wells College, 201
Wesleyan Female College, 93
White House
    Arts Committee, 166
    first family in, 25
    improvements to, 226
    rebuilding of, 154
    staff at, 139
Wilson, Edith
    history of, 123
    after husband's death, 125
    influencing Bill of Rights, 126
    odd facts about, 124
    portraits of, 117, 122
    against suffrage, 124
Wilson, Ellen
    as artist, 120–21
    health of, 121
    history of, 119
    portraits of, 117–18
Wilson, Woodrow, 119–25
Wollstonecraft, Mary, 26
women
    fighting for, 8
    first college for, 51
    first historians on, 26
    first hospital for, 68
    Global Issues of, 210
    as governors, 134
    Home Missionary Society for, 94
    in Ivy Leagues, 175
    laws for, 23–24
    as lawyers, 94
    Little Women, 86
    married, property laws for, 60
    as mayors, 102
    in military, 186

National Hall of Fame for, 188
National Organization for, 175
in Public Service Project, 210
shelter for, 109
U.S.-Afghan Women's Council for, 218
as voters, 90, 123, 140
wearing pants, 200
women's rights
    Carter, R., working for, 191–92
    spark of, 60
women voters
    first four states allowing, 102
    first state allowing, 90
    League of, 123, 140
    McKinley, I., supporting, 109
    suffrage movement start for, 78
Woodhull, Victoria, 90
World Economic Forum, 219
Wyoming, 134